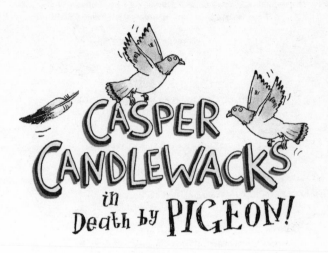

First published in Great Britain by HarperCollins *Children's Books* 2011
HarperCollins *Children's Books* is a division of HarperCollins*Publishers* Ltd,
77-85 Fulham Palace Road, Hammersmith, London W6 8JB

Visit us on the web at
www.harpercollins.co.uk

1

CASPER CANDLEWACKS IN DEATH BY PIGEON!
Text copyright © Ivan Brett 2011
Illustrations copyright © Hannah Shaw 2011

Ivan Brett asserts the moral right to be identified as the author of this work.

ISBN 978-0-00-741155-9

Printed and bound in England by
Clays Ltd, St Ives plc

Mixed Sources
Product group from well-managed
forests and other controlled sources
www.fsc.org Cert no. SW-COC-001806
© 1996 Forest Stewardship Council

FSC is a non-profit international organisation established to promote the
responsible management of the world's forests. Products carrying the FSC
label are independently certified to assure consumers that they come
from forests that are managed to meet the social, economic and
ecological needs of present and future generations.

Find out more about HarperCollins and the environment at
www.harpercollins.co.uk/green

CASPER CANDLEWACKS
in Death by PIGEON!

Ivan
Brett

Illustrated by Hannah Shaw

HarperCollins *Children's Books*

For Betty Woons, and all who tread on her

Chapter 0

A Village of Idiots

Most villages have an idiot. The village of Corne-on-the-Kobb has hundreds. I'm not just saying that; it really is full of them. I can't explain why; it's not as if there's a humungous sign as you enter saying

ONLY IDIOTS WELCOME HERE!

It's not as if there's anything particularly idiotic in the village that attracts them there, apart from other idiots, of course. It's just a fact: there is a higher concentration of idiots in Corne-on-the-Kobb than in other, less idiotically populated areas.

"But," you might ask, "what exactly *is* an idiot?" Well, the answer is as simple as the idiots themselves. An idiot is someone who talks at the people on the telly and wonders why they don't respond; someone who thinks the world's gone all dark every time they close their eyes; someone who thinks Shepherd's Pie is made of real shepherds. You get the idea. But shepherds and their pies aside, Corne-on-the-Kobb isn't exactly famous for its geniuses. Keep this fact safely stuffed inside your brain at all times when reading this tale – it might make the whole thing just that little bit easier to understand.

Of course, there is an exception to every rule, and in this case the exception's name is Casper Candlewacks. He isn't an idiot, which is really lucky because, by some strange stroke of fate, he turns out to be the hero of the story, and no one wants an idiot as their main character, do they? Well, they might, but their story would end rather soon, with the hero glued to the ceiling or dangling off a cliff, and that wouldn't make for a very good book.

Chapter 1

The Odd One Out

This was it. His moment.

"Casper."

He stood, rapier blade in hand, face to face with the vile beast. Their eyes locked; the air around them fell still.

"Casper?" It bared its savage teeth, tail flickering menacingly, but Casper was ready. And then, it pounced.

"Casper Candlewacks, wAKE UP!"

Casper awoke with a snort and shot upright, losing his balance and sending books and pens flying across the classroom as he tipped too far backward and clattered, along with his chair, to the floor. The rest of Class 6 exploded with riotous laughter, but Mrs Snagg was less than amused.

"How *dare* you sleep in my classroom!" yelled Casper's teacher, her spiky hair bristling threateningly.

"I'm awake, miss!"

"Well, *stay awake,* boy," shouted Mrs Snagg, "or I'll glue your eyelids open myself."

"Sorry, miss." Casper was too embarrassed to want to get up ever again. The class giggled and someone threw a rubber at him.

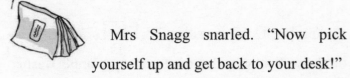

Mrs Snagg snarled. "Now pick yourself up and get back to your desk!"

Casper did as he was told, blushing like an embarrassed plum and wishing he were still asleep. He plonked himself at his desk as his classmates sniggered and pointed, and slumped his head in his hands. He was awake again: back in the boring old world full of idiots, homework and falling off chairs.

Casper Candlewacks was an eleven-year-old boy with a wild imagination and a scruffy crop of wild blond hair in which many pencils and woodland creatures had been lost. He liked log flumes, goblins and helicopter gunships. He didn't like girls, geography, or killer robots. His favourite food was spaghetti bolognese with chips, and his favourite animal was an ocelot. In other words, he was a pretty ordinary boy by our standards. But that was the problem. In a village where *ordinary* was thinking that eggs came from eggplants, Casper Candlewacks was far from ordinary. The people of Corne-on-the-Kobb didn't like Casper because he was different. He could do joined-up handwriting, he knew his times tables, he even understood French. Those things scared the villagers, and so they either ignored Casper or blamed him for things.

Casper twizzled a finger in his hair and looked out of the window. It was the dawn of summer: the sun was out, the flowers were in bloom and the little lambs were frolicking in faraway grassy meadows like tiny frolicking flumps of wool in a massive salad. But Thursday afternoons meant double geography, and so summer would have to wait.

"Now, class," squawked Mrs Snagg, rapping the board rubber loudly on her desk, making a bang so shocking that little Teresa Louncher let out a terrified squeak. Casper watched his teacher, Mrs Snagg, as she surveyed the classroom. She reminded Casper of a hedgehog in a flowery dress. She had little black beady eyes that were always watching you when you thought they weren't, and a voice like a fire alarm. Not even one of those new soothing fire alarms that play nice relaxing ditties about how great it'll be once you escape the burning building, oh no. Mrs Snagg's voice was like an old-fashioned screechy fire alarm that made your eardrums give up on hearing and apply for a job in your pancreas, where it's quieter and there's a better pension plan. She liked to fill in other people's crosswords with the wrong words in permanent pen, and she hated all boys, especially ones called Casper Candlewacks.

Now that Mrs Snagg had the attention of the class,

she continued. "Today, instead of geography, we've got a very special art class. Now I'm sure you're all awfully excited about The Great Tiramisu's visit to our village tomorrow night, so to celebrate, we'll be drawing pictures of him to put on the wall!"

Casper groaned. But for the rest of the children of Class 6, this announcement was about as exciting as disco-dancing squirrels. Celebratory cheers rang out, fireworks were let off and some small children were thrown into the air.

"Drawing instead of joglaphy? This is better than Christmiss!" declared a buoyant Ted Treadington.

Teresa Louncher was equally excited. "I'm gunna draw him with felt-tips!" she said.

For Casper, life had reached its lowest possible point. Normally, drawing would be a brilliant replacement for any real schoolwork, but even the most sleepifyingly dull geography lesson seemed better than having to draw that wand-wielding, pizza-guzzling fop. The Great Tiramisu was all that anyone had talked about for weeks, and it was getting right on Casper's nerves. Yes, he could pull a badger out of a hat, but who couldn't? And of course he had once made the entire population of Norway disappear, and reappear in Belgium, but who wants to see that anyway? Certainly not the Belgians – they didn't have enough space or waffles to go round, and the whole thing ended in quite a considerable war. Casper had seen The Great Tiramisu on TV – he was snooty, arrogant and his hair was too shiny. He said things like "*Mamma Mia!*" and applauded himself after each magic trick. Everything from his long, swizzly moustache to his cheesy Italian accent annoyed Casper almost enough to put him off a bowl of cheesy Italian spaghetti bolognese with chips. How could no one else see that? The villagers of Corne-on-the-Kobb loved The Great Tiramisu like he was giving out free chocolate cake, and it just didn't make sense. Casper solemnly refused to spend the next two hours drawing someone he'd much rather spend the next two hours firing angry gerbils at, with an angry gerbil gun.

"What's wrong, Casper?" said the class bully and teacher's pet, Anemonie Blight, who was already halfway through her pink drawing, entitled 'The Grate Terimisew'. "Forgotten how to use your hands?" The other girls laughed, but not because it was funny. If you didn't laugh at one of Anemonie's jokes, she'd probably bite you later.

Casper's face went red. "No, I just don't want to draw him, that's all."

"Miss! Miss!" cried Anemonie.

Mrs Snagg, angered after being distracted from her copy of *Hunks in Trunks* by some whingeing, snotty-faced child, saw that it was Anemonie Blight and smiled as sweetly as her sour old face would let her.

"What's bothering you, my huggypumpkin?"

"Casper isn't doing the work, miss." Anemonie shot a dirty look over at Casper, which stung as it hit him. "He's not drawing The Great Tiramisu."

Mrs Snagg peered poisonously at Casper with her little beady eyes. "Is this true, boy?"

"No, miss." Casper looked down at his blank piece of paper. "I'm just… drawing him in white."

"That's a lie, miss," said Anemonie. "He said the work was stupid and he hated drawing and then he hit me and stole my pink pencil."

"What? I didn't!"

Mrs Snagg drew in a deep breath and puffed up her chest. "Too good for drawing, are we, Candlewacks? In that case, you'll write five pages on why The Great Tiramisu is such a wonderful man and an inspiration to us all."

Anemonie and the others guffawed, as Casper recoiled from the blow. "But, miss—" he started.

"Shut up!" said Mrs Snagg, her shrill tones reverberating nauseatingly around the classroom like the screech of a badly played clarinet. "You start writing."

Casper turned to look at Anemonie. He despised that little brat, with her long brown hair and squinty eyes, and that little pointy nose just like her mother's. She had corrected her title to 'The Grait Tiremesoo', and was now defacing Teresa Louncher's drawing with her scissors and eyeliner pencil. Casper didn't think he was too good for drawing. He loved drawing good stuff, like log flumes, goblins and helicopter gunships. But The Great Tiramisu wasn't good stuff, and he didn't deserve to be drawn.

The clock had ticked itself along happily, like a time bomb, but in the other direction and with no explosions. In the last two hours Casper had climbed Mount Kilimanjaro, slain a fire-breathing dragon and landed a fighter plane behind enemy lines, but he had

most definitely not finished his work. Most of Class 6 were adding the finishing touches to their pictures. Anemonie Blight looked most proud of her creation (she had used eyeliner and lip gloss, with dried pasta for the legs), but Lamp Flannigan, who had forgotten the legs completely, was now frantically taping on an extra piece of paper to make space for them. So when Mrs Snagg rose from her desk and shouted "Time's up!" Casper looked at the clock, and then down at his paper, and then up at the clock again, and then down at his paper again, with horror. He'd written two and a half words! They were good words, but that didn't matter. 'I like Th' was not five pages. It wasn't even close, unless he had written in really big writing, or used tiny paper, but he hadn't done either. If Mrs Snagg saw that he hadn't completed his punishment, he'd be in all flavours of trouble.

Casper scoured his desk for anything that might pass for his completed punishment. Finding a piece of last week's homework, he scrubbed out the title ('Where is Brazil, and Why?') and replaced it with 'Why The Great Tiramisu is such a wonderful man and an inspiration to us all'. Casper shuffled to the front of the class and handed the paper to Mrs Snagg. The whole class went silent – silent as a mouse that had lost its voice and didn't even have anything to say anyway. Anemonie stopped pulling Teresa Louncher's hair for a moment and watched intently.

Mrs Snagg pored over the first page, blinking slowly. (She couldn't actually read, so she just pretended to.) She turned the paper over, nodded and put a little tick next to a map of Brazil. She skipped to the third page, and then the fourth, and then stopped, and looked up quizzically at Casper.

"Didn't I say five pages, Candlewacks?"

Casper looked down at his work and swallowed. His homework was only four pages long. "Miss, I…"

"And how many did you write?" Mrs Snagg's spiky face grew redder, her whole upper body began to prickle.

"Four, miss."

"And what do we say about laziness, Candlewacks?" An onlooker might have been worried that this woman was about to explode all over the room, or at least puncture and deflate like a soggy balloon.

"Miss…"

"What do we say?" spat Mrs Snagg, face now an impressive shade of purple.

Casper's stomach knotted with embarrassment as he mumbled out the much-repeated rhyme: "'Lazy boys will get no toys; idle girls won't marry Earls', miss."

"And you," she pointed her grubby old finger at Casper, "are lazy. You'll write me ten pages on 'Why I will neither get any toys nor marry any Earls', for tomorrow morning."

This was incredibly unfair. "Miss!" said Casper. "This is incredibly unfair."

"Don't answer back," Mrs Snagg shook as she shouted. "Fifteen pages."

"What?"

"Fine, Twenty."

"I didn't even—"

"Twenty-five! Now go!"

Chapter 2

Lamp Flannigan

Corne-on-the-Kobb is a lovely little village. It has a
church, a park, a school and a restaurant. There's a
pub, a shop and a flock of tame pigeons in the village
square. But hidden away from real life, in the valley of
the River Kobb, there's not much reason to go there.

In fact, no one goes to Corne-on-the-Kobb unless they live there or they've got a faulty satnav.

Casper Candlewacks had decided long ago that he didn't like living in Corne-on-the-Kobb. It was boring and tiring and lonely, and there were never any adventures to be had. Sometimes Casper thought about moving abroad, to Turkey, Thailand, or even Tunbridge Wells, but then he thought about the food and the tigers, and decided against it.

Casper trudged home dejectedly. I don't know if you've ever seen someone trudge dejectedly, but it's not a gainly sight. It's all arms and legs and huffs. Corne-on-the-Kobb was pretty today, in the sun, but Casper didn't notice. He felt horrible. That, he thought to himself, was probably the second worst day of school he'd ever had (after that one with the penguins). Twenty-five pages! For what? He trudged through the village square, past the weathered statue of Sir Gossamer D'Glaze with his glittering bejewelled sword, and past the pigeons (who were merrily pecking at a DO NOT FEED THE PIGEONS sign).

"'Ere, Casperr." It was Sandy Landscape, Corne-on-the-Kobb's 'Second Best Gardener of the Year' for twenty years running and then 'First Best Gardener of the Year' for another twelve, after the other chap got eaten by a Venus Flytrap. It's a dangerous business, gardening.

"Oh, hello, Mr Landscape," Casper replied. Sandy Landscape was the last thing he needed on an afternoon where all he really wanted to do was trudge.

"You 'aven't seen a goat runnin' about, 'av yer? 'E's about this high, brown 'air, grey beard, looks a bit like a goat."

Casper surveyed the square. "No, sorry. Haven't seen one. Is he yours?"

"Oh, no, 'e's not moine. 'E's jus' been munchin' on my geraniums. Gonner teach 'im a lesson on mannerrs." And with that, Sandy Landscape galloped away out of sight, giving the occasional call of "'Ere goaty goaty!"

Casper watched him disappear, and then got back to his trudging. He trudged past the shop and didn't even go inside for a packet of crisps. He trudged through the park, where a flustered-looking woman was being chased by a goat, and turned right at the end to trudge down Feete Street, at which point he stopped trudging. Taped to a postbox in front of him was a poster for The Great Tiramisu. There he stood, moustache glistening, with his shiny purple suit and top hat, and a smarmy smirk that said, "I'm better than you in every possible way." He was in the process of waving his magic wand at an oversized pack of cards. Casper read the little blurb beside the picture:

> *On the back of his award-winning, sell-out World Tour, Italy's most talented, beautiful and generally fabulous magician will be coming to YOUR village to baffle, amaze and inspire you with his one-of-a-kind magic extravaganza! Have*

you ever seen a levitating lion? Have you ever seen a man transform into a bowl of raspberry jelly? Neither has The Great Tiramisu, but he's working on it...

Casper sighed. Why did everyone like The Great Tiramisu so much? He was just a tacky illusionist with a crush on his own reflection and a sell-out world tour.

"I don't like him either," said Lamp Flannigan.

Casper jumped about two metres in the air. "Agh! Lamp! I've told you not to do that!"

"Not do what?"

"Not to creep up on me! It's… well… it's creepy!"

The boy looked down at his feet (which had a sponge attached to each sole) and said, "Sorry, Casper. I didn't mean to." He walked a few steps away, turned and making as much noise he could (which wasn't much, given the sponge shoes) he stomped back towards Casper. "Is that better?"

"It's a bit late now, Lamp, you've already shocked me."

Lamp Flannigan was an idiot. Of all the idiots in Class 6, Lamp was the most idiotic. He was such an idiot that even the residents of Corne-on-the-Kobb thought it, and if a group of idiots think you're an idiot, you've probably got a thing or two to worry about up there. Lamp was such an idiot that he couldn't even spell the word 'a'. He couldn't tie his shoelaces and he thought babies grew on trees. He always wore his trousers back-to-front, he was scared of trains… you get the point. Lamp was short, chunky and had a warm face with wide, vacant green eyes. He had dark scruffy hair that looked like he'd lent it to a chimney sweep for a while, and a bulbous nose that dongled downwards, like a big, ripe, nose-coloured pear with nostrils.

Lamp liked inventing things. He spent most of his time at the Kobb Valley rubbish tip where he trawled the place for driveshafts and gearboxes. He then took them all home, stuck them together with wood glue, and wondered why they didn't work. Lamp had built wind-powered space rockets, underwater helicopters and bicycles for dogs. The villagers of Corne-on-the-Kobb didn't try to stop him; after all, it wasn't hurting anyone (apart from the cycling dog, who escaped with minor bruises and a fear of handlebars). Amazingly, none of Lamp's inventions had had much success. If you're wondering about the sponge shoes, they were his invention too. They were designed for walking on water.

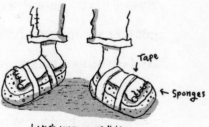

LAMP'S INVENTIONS #46
Sponge Shoes

"Can we walk home together?" said Lamp.

"Lamp, you live *that* way." Casper pointed in the direction of Lamp's house, the opposite way down the street.

Poor Lamp Flannigan was confused. He waited for a moment, and then said, "Can we walk home together?"

Casper rolled his eyes. "Fine, come on."

As they walked, Lamp told Casper about his latest invention. "It's a motorised buggy, but it runs on washing-up liquid. You know – what you wash dishes with. I haven't got it working yet because I haven't got any washing-up liquid, but I'll find some soon. And it sits two people, so when it's finished we can drive around town, you and me!"

"I've got to do that punishment tonight, Lamp. I can't go on your buggy until it's finished." He didn't want to go on Lamp's buggy at all because he valued having his limbs still attached to his body, but the punishment was a good excuse.

Lamp chuckled and carried on. "That's all right, I understand. Mrs Snagg was mean to you today. She's mean to everyone. Apart from Enemy."

Casper looked at Lamp quizzically. "Enemy?"

"Yeah, Emenemy," said Lamp.

"Anemonie?"

He tried again. "Emenony."

"Anemonie!"

"Aminime?"

They walked in silence for a bit, turning the corner into Cracklin Crescent, where Casper lived.

"Are you going to see The Great Tyrannosaurus then?" asked Lamp.

Casper shook his head. "No, I can't stand him. He

thinks he's better than everyone else, but he's not."

"I don't really understand magic," said Lamp, "but my mum got me a ticket. She says I should take up other hobbies, not just inventing. I told her there was no point because I'm going to be a famous inventor and I'm going to invent the self-cleaning armchair, but she doesn't care."

"The self-cleaning armchair?"

"I know! Why has nobody thought of it before? Anyway, do you want to come with me? Mum got another ticket for a friend and you're my best friend." Casper was Lamp's best friend, whether he liked it or not.

However much Casper hated the idea of going, he really didn't want to hurt Lamp's feelings either. "OK. I suppose I'll come with you."

Lamp grinned.

"But no inventions, all right?"

Lamp's grin faded. "I was going to wear my glow-in-the-dark trousers!"

Lamp's glow-in-the-dark trousers were just a pair of back-to-front jeans with a torch stuck on each leg.

Back to front

← Tape

Torches →

LAMP'S INVENTIONS #83
Glow in the dark trousers

Casper looked worried. "I'm not sure that would be the best idea."

"Fine," said Lamp. "Not the trousers. Got it."

By this time, the two boys had reached Casper's front door. Casper could hear screeching from inside, followed by a loud bump, a howl and the smashing of glass.

"I think I'd better get inside."

"Can I come in?"

"Not today, Lamp, I've got that punishment to do."

41

"Okey-dokey. See you tomorrow." Lamp waved and sponged off down the road. Then he stopped, turned round and sponged back in the other direction. He stopped again, scratched his head and looked back at Casper.

"That way." Casper pointed in the direction of Lamp's house. As Lamp walked off, Casper opened the door and made his way in, ducking just in time to avoid the orange glob of unidentified flying baby food that flew past his head and splatted on the wall behind him. "Great," groaned Casper. "Feeding time."

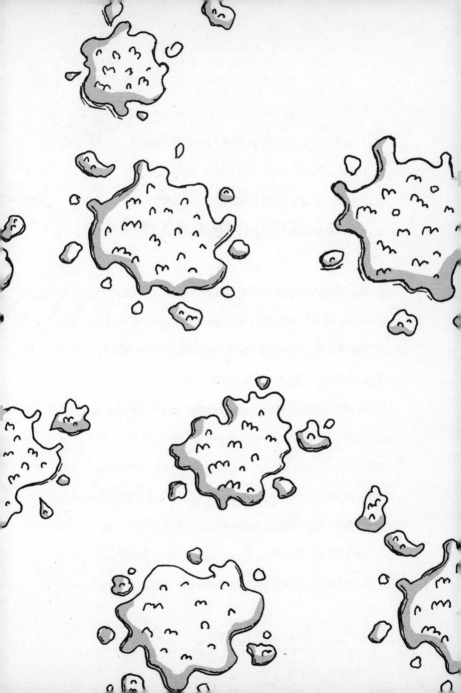

Chapter 3

Meet the Candlewackses

In this chapter, I'd like to talk to you about the mating patterns of Indonesian Wasps. But, given that the title is 'Meet The Candlewackses', that's probably a bad idea. Perhaps there'll be space for it later.

Casper dreaded coming home, every single day. It's not that school was much better, but at least there he could get some sleep. Home was just horrible. First, there was his mum, Amanda Candlewacks. Amanda was once the most beautiful young woman in the Kobb Valley. She had flowing, golden hair that shone in the sun like radioactive noodles. She wore dresses made of pure, hand-woven silk and rode around on the back of a magical oversized butterfly. But then she married Casper's father, they had their first little blond-haired baby, and it all went a bit wrong. Life got too stressful for Amanda and her escape was television. At first, she just watched the soaps. She'd track the goings-on of the folks down at *Rudgebunkle Farm* like there was a test on it afterwards. Then she got into the hospital dramas, and the knitting shows, and the late-night high stakes games of *Hungry Hungry Hippos*. Soon she wouldn't miss a second of any of the sit-coms, even *My Sister's a Llama* and *Mates?!*. Now she practically lived on that sofa, only getting up at advert breaks. She watched *How Clean is your Face?* and *Cooking with Dinosaurs*, sometimes *The World's Funniest Nostrils* and always *Whose Flan?* Her once flowing, golden hair now resembled a

dirty handful of dry straw, and she hadn't ridden on the back of any magical oversized butterflies for years.

The poor woman was addicted to that telly like Betty Woons was addicted to jelly beans.

Casper's dad, Julius Candlewacks, had to cook, clean, sweep, mop and dust. He had to do all the washing, get the weekly shopping and tend to his rapidly receding hairline. Add to that his job, head chef at The Boiled Sprout – the best (and worst) restaurant in Corne-on-the-Kobb – and the eight- month-old baby that he had to raise, Julius's life was about as hellish as sticking your tongue in a hole punch. Casper was glad he didn't have his dad's life (or his hairline), but he did feel sorry for the man. He'd not had a day off for years, didn't have any spare time for friends or sleep, and he hardly even spoke to

Casper unless he was asking for help with the baby.

But it gets worse because this was no ordinary baby. This was Cuddles Candlewacks. Cuddles liked kicking, screaming and being sick and nothing else – except for biting. It loved biting. Cuddles was a tiny terror of a tiddler with six tremendous teeth, and preferred gnawing on people rather than cuddling them. Its teeth were razor-sharp, more like fangs, really, and it wasn't afraid to use them. Audrey Snugglepuss, after trying to pat Cuddles on the head, lost her left thumb. She can no longer play the trombone (which, to be honest, is a relief).

Casper had never noticed whether Cuddles was a boy or a girl, but it didn't really matter; its teeth would be just as sharp either way. Cuddles was just… Cuddles. Amanda had never taken any notice of Cuddles at all because it wasn't on TV. Worst of all,

since the last babysitter was admitted to hospital with multiple stab wounds and first-degree burns, when Julius went out to work every evening, Casper had to babysit.

"Hi, Dad," Casper shouted. He stood in the cluttered hall next to an overturned pot plant. On his left was the darkened living room, where Amanda was slouched in her pyjamas, watching three pots of yoghurt splat about the screen. "Hi, Mum."

No reply.

"Anything good on?"

"Shhh," said Amanda, "this is a good bit."

Casper walked past the stairs on his right, avoiding the patch of sick on the carpet, to the kitchen, where his father was overseeing Cuddles painting its face with its dinner. Julius was quite tall, with dark thinning hair and small ears. He wore a grubby chef's jacket covered in sticky stains and crumbly bits, over a pair of mucky brown trousers that, years ago, used to be white. His chin was stubbly and unshaven and there were heavy bags under his eyes (eye bags, not shopping bags, you idiot). The poor man hadn't had a full night of sleep since the day Cuddles was born.

"Come on, Cuddles. Eat this spoonful for Daddy…" pleaded Julius, prodding a plastic spoon towards the baby. Cuddles grabbed the spoon and flung it back at Julius, cackling with delight.

Casper surveyed the revolting mess that was the kitchen. There was baby food on the floor and quite a bit on the ceiling too. There was a massive pile of dirty pots and pans in the sink, sporting all different sorts of mould and grease, from putrid purple patches to stinking sepia slimy bits. Two smashed plates had been left on the floor next to the leftover cabbage, which a troop of hungry ants had recently invaded. They were now celebrating their victory by having a tiny ant-party with even tinier bottles of champagne and minuscule party hats.

"House needs a clean," said Casper.

A pile of newspapers on the corner of the table began to ring. Julius looked at them and frowned. They rang again. Julius blinked. "Why are they…?"

"It's the phone, Dad. Under the papers."

Casper's bedraggled father clicked his teeth and lifted the pile carelessly, strewing hundreds of issues of the *Daily Kobb* all over the kitchen floor, one particularly bulky sports section landing right on the cabbage, causing an early and tragic end to the ant-party. Not a moment too soon, Julius found the phone and answered it, while Cuddles stretched to grab the receiver with its chubby little arms.

"Hello, Candlewacks residence. Yes, speaking. It's who? Ooh…" Julius looked up, caught Casper's eye and tried frantically to mime something. He waved his arm around a bit and then put his finger on his top lip like a moustache and looked at Casper encouragingly.

"What?" said Casper. He thought his dad might have been trying to say something about cricket.

Julius mimed a sort of 'forget it' gesture and continued. "How may I help you, Mr Tiramisu, sir?"

Casper's jaw dropped.

"You'd like to… well, of course! I'd be honoured. Will you excuse me for just one second, Mr Tiramisu, I just need to attend to a… cooking thing." Julius snatched a dummy and jammed it into a wailing Cuddles's mouth, but it chomped it in half and started smacking the pieces on its tray.

Casper looked over to his dad in disbelief. "Did you say Tiramisu?"

"It's him!" Julius whispered to Casper. "He wants to eat at The Boiled Sprout!" He grinned manically and shook his fist like footballers do when they score goals, or like chefs do when famous Italian magicians want to eat at their restaurant.

"That's great!" Casper lied. It wasn't great, it was terrifying. Who knows what The Great Tiramisu would demand, but whatever it was, Julius wouldn't be able to do it. And then what would happen…?

Julius whispered again, "Get me a pen and paper, quick!"

Cuddles launched again for the phone, but completely missed and almost toppled its high chair. It let out a frustrated screech and then distracted itself by gnawing on a mouthful of its own fingers.

Returning to the phone call, Julius said, "Sorry, Mr Tiramisu, I had to put the finishing touches to a dish. A scream? No, I don't think… oh yes, one of my sous-chefs. Child? Well, I like to hire them when they're young. So, ahem, is there anything you'd like

to eat in particular?" Just in time, Casper handed his
dad the pad of paper and he scrawled frantically,

 Tiramisu
Tomorrow, after show
Finest Food
IMPORTANT: NO CORIANDER

... and then Cuddles got its greedy little hand to the
phone, grabbed it, threw it at the wall and it smashed
into hundreds of little phoney pieces.

All the Facts That Exist About Coriander.

Coriander was first discovered in 1834 by Sir Digmund Coriander-Discoverer, when he was looking in his garden for a little something to add flavour to his carrot soup. He tried adding grass, but it tasted too lawny; so next he tried some bark, but it tasted too tree-ey. Then he noticed, nestling amongst the lupins, a mysterious aromatic herb. He put some in his soup and the rest, as they say, is cookery.

Here are some fun facts about coriander that you may or may not know:

In some countries, coriander is used for medicinal purposes, such as in Burma, where it is the accepted treatment for a cracked rib.

A particularly leafy sprig of coriander won the 1997 Oscar for 'Best Herb in a Supporting Role' in the film *Coriander and Me*.

The small English village of Upper Crustenbury, in the picturesque Kobb Valley, is famous for its bountiful coriander crops; so much so that its residents hold an annual coriander festival to celebrate their favourite herb.

The word 'coriander' comes from the Romanian, *Quarie ain derr*, which, due to a small translation error, literally means 'A small, sticky badger with a pair of shorts on its head'.

Famous Italian magician 'The Great Tiramisu' is violently allergic to coriander. If he eats even the smallest amount, his face inflates and turns green and he breaks out in big oozing yellow pustules. Because of this, he telephones ahead of his visit to any restaurant to ask specifically that no coriander be added to his food.

These are all the facts that exist about coriander. If anyone tells you any more coriander facts, they are lying and should be pelted with rotten quinces. If you don't have any quinces to hand, a handful of chopped apricots will do fine.

Chapter 4

What Casper Saw

The whole village had turned out to see The Great Tiramisu, apart from Julius, Cuddles and Amanda Candlewacks, and the one-hundred-and-seven-year-old Betty Woons, who had hated magic ever since her husband was killed by a wild pack of cards. Everyone else was there, even the village mascot, Fatima the ferret, who was sitting in her cage in the front row nibbling on a vole. The magic show was nearing an end, and even Casper had quite enjoyed it, apart from the fact that Lamp Flannigan had taken the 'no glow-in-the-dark trousers' comment to mean no trousers at all, which had caused great embarrassment for Casper and hilarity for Anemonie and chums. Lamp thought all the laughing was a good thing, so he made some manly poses and showed off his legs, none of which made it any better.

The Great Tiramisu's grand finale involved locking a volunteer, giggly little Teresa Louncher, in an underwater metal cage, and then impaling her with two sharpened (but rather bewildered) swordfish. The swordfish were removed, the cage was lifted out of the water, the magic wand was waved and Teresa sprang back to life, screeching with delight. At this point the audience in the village hall erupted with

tumultuous applause like a really impressed volcano.

"He's utterly delightful!" screamed Audrey Snugglepuss, village gossip and vice-chairwoman of the Corne-on-the-Kobb Carrot Cake Appreciation

Society, from behind Casper.

"An' so good wiv swordfish," said Sandy Landscape, "but how'd 'e do that there one with the cheese and the dynamite?" (If you're interested, he had a hidden mirror behind the walrus. Simple, really.)

It was most certainly a standing ovation. If there were an even better ovation than a standing one, like a jumping ovation or something, it would have been that. For the idiots of Corne-on-the-Kobb, Christmas and Birthday and Halloween and even Saint Pelican's Day had come all at once, in the shape of a moustache-sporting Italian illusionist who could make bagfuls of rabbits disappear. Most of the villagers would have been impressed if he'd flipped a coin or jangled some keys, so you can imagine how amazed they were when The Great Tiramisu got cut in half, locked his legs in a safe, put that safe in another safe, put that safe in a box full of snakes, angered the snakes by insulting their mother, and then somehow unlocked the safes and glued himself together again, blindfolded, hands tied behind his back, while asleep.

"I thank-a you all, you beautiful people! Wasn't I *magnifico*!" sang the magician, as some of the women near the front threw bunches of freshly picked dandelions and salad leaves at his feet. Mayor Rattsbulge, Corne-on-the-Kobb's fattest mayor since the pie tax was abolished, managed to lift his hefty frame on stage to thank The Great Tiramisu personally and to offer him the key to the village (which he accepted reluctantly because he hadn't a clue what it was for) along with a bouquet of summer roses presented by Anemonie Blight in a sickly pink frock and matching hairband. Yes, The Great Tiramisu was a show-off of the vilest proportions, but Casper had to admit that his magic tricks had actually been quite good.

As the excited idiots filed out of the village hall, Lamp, still without trousers, approached Casper eagerly. "Want to come and try my buggy? I've got some washing-up liquid now. Found it in a shop."

"I can't. I've got to take The Great Tiramisu over to the restaurant, and then I've got to help with the cooking. Maybe another time?"

"Oh, brill! Can I help?"

"I don't need any help, Lamp."

"Great! Let's go." Lamp rubbed his hands together with excitement.

"Didn't you hear what I said?"

"Come on, don't want to keep him waiting," said Lamp, and he gallumphed off in the direction of the dressing room. Casper sighed and hurried off after him.

As the boys neared the dressing room, Casper noticed that the door had been left ajar, and from inside wafted indistinct sounds of shouting, stomping and perhaps a smattering of splattering. "Shh, listen. What's that?" Casper whispered, creeping closer. Silently they peered through the crack in the door, and saw, well…

What would you say was the least likely thing that Casper and Lamp would have seen inside that room? Giant kung-fu-fighting gooseberries? The Philharmonic Hedge-Trimmer Orchestra of Hull? The Twelve Labours of Hercules lovingly sculpted out of one massive slab of milk chocolate? If you happened to say any of these things, give yourself ten points and a biscuit because you weren't that far off. Through the gap they saw The Great Tiramisu, parading furiously up and down in front of a trembling line of circus animals, all dressed in purple velvet bow ties, purple top hats and fake moustaches. There were three white rabbits, a walrus, a Shetland pony, a majestic white tiger, at least a dozen doves, two swordfish in a tank and a whole host of attending beavers that Casper swore he hadn't even seen in the show.

"*Terribile! Orrendo! Abominevole!*" The Great Tiramisu raved. "I have seen performing vegetables better than-a you." He picked up a vase and threw it at the wall; it shattered, casting glass shards into the flock of doves, who flapped about in panic.

Casper caught his breath. He watched the Shetland pony let out a terrified whinny.

"You!" continued The Great Tiramisu, pointing at the walrus. "You think I pay you to slouch around like-a the tower of Pisa? I tell you to do-a the jig. Why you no do-a the jig?"

The walrus shrugged.

"Do not look at-a me, you *imbecille*! You are ugly and smell of the fish."

Crumpling his nose, the walrus barked and covered his eyes with a damp flipper. Outside the door Casper was stunned and horrified. He couldn't believe the cruelty he was seeing.

"And-a the birdies!" The magician wheeled around to face the doves, who fluttered anxiously. "You think you-a the pigeons? The flippy-flappy picky-pecky pigeons?"

The doves looked at each other and then back at The Great Tiramisu and nodded.

"NO!" exploded The Great Tiramisu, seething, flecks of spit flying from his mouth like a hosepipe with a blockage. "You bird-brained *idioti*! You-a no flippy-flappy picky-pecky. You need-a the grace, the style, like-a me. *Mamma Mia!* I will bake you in a *calzone*, you dirty fowl."

Casper felt sick. How could The Great Tiramisu be so vile to those animals? He noticed tears welling up in Lamp's eyes.

The Great Tiramisu stomped towards the white tiger, who cowered away from his towering gait and trembling moustache. "And you," he scowled, his bottom lip quivering with fury. "You-a de fool of a pussycat. You do what I say, and I say-a card tricks. You no doo-a the card tricks? I shave-a naughty words in your fur! I pluck out your whiskers and knit them into my hat! I… I…" The Great Tiramisu heard a sob from just outside his door. "Hello? Who's there?"

The door creaked open and Casper stepped in, flushed red, but desperately restraining his anger. Lamp, teary-eyed, trouserless and whimpering into a hanky, took one more look at the downtrodden animals and fled, wailing all the way along the corridor.

"What do you want?" said The Great Tiramisu, brushing himself down.

Casper's hands were shaking; he could hardly hold it in. He wanted to throttle that Italian bully. "I'm supposed to take you to the restaurant," he said, as calmly as he could.

"About time too. I thought you 'ad forgotten me." He threw on a purple cape, ushered Casper briskly out of the room and slammed the door behind him.

The animals heaved a sigh of relief. The Shetland pony lay down, exhausted, and the beavers and rabbits crowded round her for a cuddle. The two swordfish nuzzled each other and the white tiger licked the walrus to keep it moist.

Chapter 5

 # The Coriander Catastrophe

Casper played over in his head the events he'd just witnessed. He was right about The Great Tiramisu all along; what a cruel, conceited man. Casper hated him, all the way from his shiny purple shoes to his bristling moustache. But as they walked towards The Boiled Sprout, he could do nothing about it.

"I will have-a the best table," The Great Tiramisu demanded. "I will expect my food at once and it will-a be hot. Are-a we clear?"

"Yes, sir." Casper clenched his fists.

"And-a *no coriander*!"

"No, sir, no coriander."

As they approached The Boiled Sprout, Casper could see that either word had spread about The Great Tiramisu's dining arrangements or everyone in the village suddenly yearned for a plate of broiled gristle with claggy sauce because the place was positively bulging. Reaching the restaurant door, The Great Tiramisu halted, adjusted his top hat, twizzled his moustache and said, "You will announce me."

Casper choked. "What?"

"Enter first and announce me. *Now!*"

What barefaced cheek! Casper wanted nothing more than to turn round and knock off The Great Tiramisu's top hat, but he bit his tongue and pushed open the door. The restaurant fell silent; silent as a mouse in a game of hide-and-squeak. (The hiding mouse, not the squeaking one.)

"Ladies and Gentlemen," began Casper, blood rushing hot through his veins, "The Great Ti—"

"Yes! It is me!" The Great Tiramisu strode in, cape a-flutter, arms out in appreciation. The restaurant went nuts, cheering, whooping and showering him with a confetti of boiled rice. Casper felt a rough shove.

"Go away," The Great Tiramisu whispered, "you-a ruin my moment."

With that, Casper stomped into the kitchen, red-faced and angry, where Julius was more stressed than Father Christmas would be on Christmas Eve if all the elves went down with reindeer flu. The sausages under the grill were on fire, something in a pan was bubbling over and the mashed potato was producing a pungent blackish smoke. The counter was covered in thick yellow foam. There were teetering piles of dirty pots, pans, trays, cockroaches and

underpants. There was a basin full of used knives and forks covered in a greasy glunch, and a rat, perched on a plate, feasting on some abandoned aubergine curry.

Julius had had no choice but to bring Cuddles to work with him, so he'd stuck it to the wall with parcel tape to keep it out of the way. It was perfectly happy up there, screeching every so often and spitting in passing plates of chips.

"Is that him?" asked Julius, frantically scraping the green bits off some pork chops.

"Yeah," Casper grunted. "Aren't we lucky." His mind flitted back to those poor animals, treated like slaves, and another wave of anger surged up within him.

"He'll be expecting his terrine," said Julius,

slipping on a gravy puddle. He cursed and threw a pan full of scorched egg at the sink, which missed and hit the floor with a resounding clang. As he ran to clear it up he slipped again on the gravy, this time falling and hitting the floor himself with a resounding thud (not a clang).

Julius Candlewacks's Oyster and Asparagus Terrine is famous around the Kobb Valley. Both a culinary delight and a strong disinfectant, the leftovers can be used to clean your toilet. Renowned French food critic Jean-Claude d'Escargot described it as being "not zat bad", a quote that Julius will proudly carry to his grave.

"WHERE IS MY DINNER?" came the shout from the restaurant. The Great Tiramisu was getting impatient.

Julius rummaged around for the note he'd written

during yesterday's phone call. "Where did I put it?" He didn't know it, but his note was simmering away happily in the chicken soup, adding a sumptuous papery tang. "What did it say? It said, ah, something about coriander… but did he want loads of it or none at all? Oh, please tell me you remember, Casper."

Casper remembered perfectly what the note said. But there's a curious thing that happens sometimes when you get angry or upset. Bits of your body get big ideas and ignore your brain; you just start running, or shouting things, or eating all the cheese in the house (even your emergency Jarlsberg). For Casper, this was one of those occasions because while his brain transmitted "*IMPORTANT: NO CORIANDER*" down the brainial tube to his voice box (and that's science), his voice box wasn't listening. It was enraged, frothing with flaming words of fury and the hot spit of revenge, and it wasn't doing requests. So without warning, as if from afar, Casper heard himself blurt, "He wanted coriander, Dad. Lots."

"Of course! I knew it," said Julius, as he ransacked his shelves for the stuff, brushing aside the pickled onions, a train timetable and an empty ketchup bottle. "I know it's here somewhere…"

Casper instantly covered his mouth with his hand. That was not supposed to come out. "Actually, I think it was…"

"I AM STILL-A WAITING!" yelled The Great Tiramisu. "CAN YOU NOT COOK?"

"No time, Casper," said Julius, frantically assembling the dish. Glad that he'd remembered Tiramisu's wish, he mixed great ladlefuls of ground coriander with the oysters, and added whole sprigs of coriander leaf to the asparagus, topping with lavish sprinklings of coriander seeds and finishing off with a liberal glug of *essence de coriander*, something of a delicacy, but not wasted on The Great Tiramisu, Julius assured himself.

Proudly, Julius lifted the plate and took a sniff. "Ooh! Coriandery! Just how he likes it."

Casper swallowed weakly; his mouth had gone dry. "No, Dad, I…"

"Shh. This is my moment!" Julius grinned at his invention and strutted into the restaurant, dramatically pushing aside the swinging doors like in a cowboy film, which prompted the expected gasp from the observing diners (and an unimpressed snort from a passing cowboy).

Casper peered through the crack in a door for the second time that night. His stomach twisted in on itself like a little black hole of worry, he felt faint and his hands were cold and clammy. What did coriander do to The Great Tiramisu? "Suppose I'm about to find out…" he muttered.

Julius brandished his dish with pride. "May I present my very own Oyster and Asparagus Terrine, with a very special twist." He placed it in front of The Great Tiramisu and stepped back. Everyone gasped again.

The Great Tiramisu examined his meal and said, "It looks-a *molto delizioso*."

The diners all went silent, silent as an even quieter mouse that has taken a vow of silence and takes that vow very seriously, and won't talk even for a billion bits of cheese. The Great Tiramisu took his fork and delicately picked out a mouthful, lifted it to his mouth and chewed thoughtfully. He swallowed, nodded and smiled to his audience. "*Bravissimo!*" he sang, and everyone joined him with a jubilant round of applause. Champagne corks popped, glasses were emptied and Clemmie Answorth fell off her chair.

Casper's heart fluttered as madly as a one-winged butterfly in a wind tunnel. Nothing was happening. Had he got away with it?

But as if on cue, before he could take another bite, something peculiar started to happen to The Great Tiramisu. He coughed and his face began to pale, first turning white, but then shading to a puce green. Little brown spots appeared on his face; he touched his cheek, but drew it away fast, looking down with terror at the terrine on his plate. As the villagers watched, the little brown spots grew into large yellow bumps. The Great Tiramisu turned to Julius, with fear in his eyes.

"M-m-my face... There was... c-c-coriander?" he

gasped. Everyone else gasped. There was a lot of gasping, by the way.

Julius was shocked. "I thought you…"

Casper winced.

"You *idiota*!" shouted The Great Tiramisu, as he staggered to his feet and threw his plate shattering to the floor. As he stood there, his greenish face began to swell and puff like an angry blowfish. He clutched his spotty cheek once more. "My face! My poor-a beautiful face!"

Anemonie Blight cackled at The Great Tiramisu and tugged on her mother's sleeve, shouting, "Mummy, look at his ugly face! He's got diseases!"

Other villagers laughed and pointed. Betty Woons got out her camera and took a picture for the *Daily Kobb*.

Too guilty to watch another moment, Casper turned

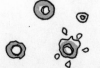

away and paced around the kitchen. He'd just done something very evil, and very, very stupid. "I'm not supposed to be evil *or* stupid, Cuddles," he sighed, clutching his forehead. "What was I doing?"

Cuddles, bound by parcel tape, cackled and banged its head against the wall.

Back in the restaurant The Great Tiramisu teetered about, top heavy, wheezing almost musically, trying to hide his bloated face from the sniggering crowd. Then one or two of the big yellow spots on his face burst, shooting sickening spats of creamy pus in all directions. Two or three of the more sensitive women fainted, and Clemmie Answorth, who had just got back on her chair, fell off again. The

Great Tiramisu's swollen face was now a vibrant grass-green and the size of a beach ball, and he was screaming things at Julius in Italian that the villagers assumed to be very rude or very insulting, or both. (It was both, by the way.) He lurched violently at Audrey Snugglepuss's helping hand before falling to his knees. Audrey shrieked and jumped back as The Great Tiramisu clattered to the floor.

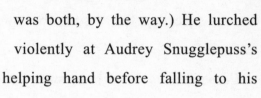

"The shame… I cannot be seen like-a this!" As more pus splurged from the yellow pustules, The Great Tiramisu tried to hide his huge green face behind his hands, but they hardly covered his bloated nostrils, let alone the rest of it.

The villagers watched, helpless. Betty Woons took another picture.

"A-a... curse," The Great Tiramisu rasped. "A curse on your *stupido* village." He coughed up something orange. "I set-a curse to you all!" and then he ran, squealing like a squealbarrow, out of the restaurant.

Casper peered through the swinging doors to see what damage he'd caused. A few final diners were rushing outside to follow the swollen-faced magician, leaving Mayor Rattsbulge shoving everyone's leftovers into his pockets (which was difficult, seeing as a lot of people had soup). A forlorn-looking Julius stared at the barely eaten terrine. Outside, a crowd of people were shouting and screaming, crying and wailing, and generally overreacting.

Julius turned round, spotted Casper and smiled feebly. "I suppose he won't be wanting his pudding then."

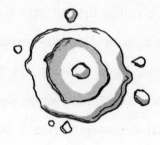

Chapter 6

Race Day

If I were to ask you to list the three things that most define what it is to be English, you'd probably say tea, cricket and donkey racing. In fact, it's been scientifically proven that the average Englishman likes nothing more than galloping round the cricket pitch on the back of a toothy steed with a nice mug of Earl Grey and a ginger biscuit.

Of course, donkey racing was invented by Lord Manfred Donkey-Racing-Inventor in July 1483, after having been chased around a bit by a flock of angry donkeys. "What fun!" he delighted, leaping over a fence, catching his foot and landing heavily on his head with a resounding clang. Inventing donkey racing was the last thing Lord Manfred Donkey-Racing-Inventor ever did, but luckily it was all embroidered by an onlooker and sent in to *"You've Been Weaved"* and the rest, as they say, is tapestry.

It was a warm Saturday afternoon, and the horrors of the previous night had faded into a cluttered memory of coriander and screaming. Today was Donkey Day, so the important thing was to move forward and put on a brave face. Betty Woons had left her brave face at home, so she just put on her surprised one and hoped no one would notice.

The donkey race was an important event in the Corne-on-the-Kobb calendar (which is the same as other calendars except that October is spelt wrong). Bean, the pub dog, had chased the pigeons away from the square, and Audrey Snugglepuss had vacuum-cleaned the roads. Sandy Landscape had laid out cones to mark the race track, with a wobbly finish line made of squirty-cream (he didn't have any real paint, and cream was the right colour). A few stalls had been set up selling the usual Donkey Day snacks: stir-fried liquorice sticks or doughnuts filled with hot mutton jam.

About an hour before the race, the villagers started to appear. Hardened old men in green cagoules and floppy brown hats stood around the makeshift paddock at the centre of the square taking bets, and excited idiots mingled about, looking for the best offers, or in Betty Woons's case, looking for her spectacles.

"Out of the six, my money's with Bunty's Lad," one man with a beard whispered to another man, with a bigger beard.

"No, no, Marzipan House has the form behind him," the beardier man replied, "and with odds of five-to-one, it's a good bet."

"You're both wrong," said a third man, whose beard was considerably beardier than both of the first two, and his moustache wasn't bad either. "I've talked to the trainers and they all say that Butterly Clasp is a sure win." The first two men scratched their beards and hurried away to place large bets on Butterly Clasp, while the third man changed his mind at the final moment and put every penny he had on McFrockles, apart from two pounds, which he saved for some beard cream.

Bunty's Lad was the clear favourite. Tall and muscular and built for racing, he brayed like a foghorn and strutted around like a mobile foghorn, flashing his shiny teeth. He was attracting the most attention from the crowd, and after he headbutted Ol' Toney, at least four people raced off to place a considerable chunk on him to win. In fact, the only donkey that wasn't looking good was Ol' Toney himself. An ageing racer, at a fine age of 96 donkey years (which is 324 hamster years, if that helps), Ol' Toney used to be the finest racing donkey in the Kobb Valley. However, after breaking all of his

legs in a horrific carrot-and-stick accident, he never returned to form. He looked tired and weak, and no one had placed a penny on the old fellow.

By the time Casper, Julius and Cuddles (tucked firmly inside Julius's backpack, with its head poking out of the top) had arrived, the square was packed as full as Mayor Rattsbulge's fridge. Casper had slept terribly; the events of last night had haunted his dreams and awoken him, shaking, in cold sweats. The Great Tiramisu deserved everything that came to him, but that didn't make it any better. Casper had lied and betrayed his dad. He looked up at Julius, who looked wearier and more run-down than ever, not helped by the fact that Cuddles had twisted round and was now trying to eat his thinning hair.

A monstrous prickling pang of guilt surged through Casper's body. Getting his own back was one thing, but he wished he could have done it a different way.

Children were climbing on Sir Gossamer D'Glaze (the statue, not the corpse) to get a better view, and it was wobbling ominously. Flurries of frantic gamblers placed final flutters on their chosen donkey, or pushed to the front of the crowd to get a good view. Audrey Snugglepuss was the first to notice Julius.

"You've got some explaining to do, young man," she said, striding towards him, waggling her bony thumb-stump. "We're a laughing stock, you know."

Sandy Landscape, who had been standing nearby kicking a flowerbed, joined in. "Arr, you done poisoned 'im up good 'n' proper," he said.

Julius's shoulders dropped. "I'm sorry, I…"

"Mummy, Mummy, look!" came a sharp, shrill

voice. "It's the food murderer!" It was that brat Anemonie Blight and her pointy mother. She puffed out her cheeks and clutched her neck. "Help! Someone help! He's poisoned me!"

Mrs Blight simpered and wrinkled her pointy nose at Julius. "Stay away from him, Nemmie. You don't know where he's been."

"It wasn't Dad's fault," said Casper, blood boiling.

"What, poison himself, did he?" said Audrey Snugglepuss.

"No," said Casper, "Dad didn't know about the allergy, that's all."

"The boy genius is telling us what we don't know now, is he?"

"I didn't mean that!"

"Come on, Casp. Just ignore them." Julius put his arm round Casper and led him away, but they followed on behind, pointing fingers and whispering.

"Hi, Casper!" called Lamp, bounding over from across the square.

Casper groaned. Lamp looked ridiculous in his blue boiler suit and pointy green hat. His hands, clothes and mouth were covered in black sticky grease. By the look of his vacant grin, he'd completely forgotten about last night.

"Sorry about my mess," Lamp drawled. "I was trying to make some edible ink, but it didn't work and I can't get it off. What are all those people looking at?"

"Nothing, Lamp. Look, I'm not in the mood for—" but at that moment the big horn sounded, announcing the arrival of Mayor Rattsbulge and Fatima the ferret. The mayor carried an extra-large bag of chips, paid for, as was all of his food, by the Corne-on-the-Kobb heritage fund. Casper, Lamp and Julius (and Cuddles,

94

noisily trying to gnaw its way out of the backpack)
hurried over to a spot near the statue, creaking under
the burden of so many children, and they waited for
the race to begin.

"Before we start," said Mayor Rattsbulge, putting aside his chips for a moment, "I bring news that will please you all. The Great Tiramisu is in a healthy and stable state after last night's… events."

"No thanks to him," said Audrey Snugglepuss with a sideways sneer at Julius.

Casper bit his lip and worried. This wasn't going well.

"That's quite enough," the mayor said, silencing the crowd. "No harm done. Now, on with the race."

The crowd cheered and switched attention to the starting line, where the six donkeys were lined up in their decorative saddles, hats and scarves. Mayor Rattsbulge opened the cage and took out a squirming Fatima. He held her up to the starting ribbon, and she did just as rehearsed and snapped it with her sharp little teeth. The race had begun! From out of the

96

highest window of the town hall, Larry Flip-Flop
commentated on the race through a megaphone

We're under starter's orders...
and they're off! The
first donkey round
three laps of the
square will be
champion. Chimney
Chap has made a good start; so
has Marzipan House and... oh dear!
Ol' Toney hasn't started. I think he's asleep! Hope
none of you put any cash on him – I could run
faster than that creaky mule. Now here comes McFrockles,
putting some serious hoof into it, passing Marzipan
House. Looks like it's clouding over now – good
news for Chimney Chap, who thrives on muggy

conditions. Ol' Toney's woken up now, but he looks tired already. We're on to the second lap... Wait, was that a spot of rain? Yep, it's definitely raining. Bad news for Butterly Clasp – she's got dry-course hooves on for this race. Oh, darn, did I leave the washing on the line? Now Bunty's Lad takes the lead and the crowd seems to like it, while Ol' Toney is having a sit-down. They've lapped him! He'll have his work cut out now. Chimney Chap is dropping back, but McFrockles slips and almost falls as the rain gets heavier. You know what, I did leave my washing out, and it's tipping it down now. It'll be soaked. Marzipan House takes second place now. We're nearing the third lap, and Ol' Toney's back in the hunt, but a good lap-and-a-half behind. But as they say, it's not over till the fat donkey sings. They say something like that, anyway. Hot favourite Bunty's Lad has put some space between himself and the pack now, but Butterly Clasp is slipping about on those wet cobbles like Clemmie Answorth after a couple of gins. Was that thunder? I'm pretty sure I just heard thunder. Chimney Chap has pricked up his ears and looks alarmed… knock me down, he's running away! Watch out, people, donkey on the loose. Oy, Mrs Woons, watch out! Watch… oh, my! Can we get a medic over there, please? Back to the race, there are… wait… two, three… carry the one… five donkeys left. I can hardly see the course 'cause of this rain. And… oh, my goodness! Butterly Clasp has slipped on a cobble. He's down! He's out of the race. I told you his dry-course hooves were a problem. Back at the front we're nearing the final turn with Bunty's Lad leading and McFrockles and Marzipan House in hot pursuit. Oh, no – another clap of thunder. But it's going to be

Bunty's Lad! He's got just metres to go... Bunty's Lad now... the crowd is going wild... he's going to do it, and... what? Did you see that? A bolt of lightning has... well, it struck Bunty's Lad! And in the confusion McFrockles and Marzipan House have clattered right into him and they've tripped over too. This is incredible! It's all down to Ol' Toney. He still has a lap to go, but he's the only donkey left. Come on, Ol' Toney! More lightning strikes, but it won't daunt Ol' Toney: he's deaf as a doorknob. He's nearing the final corner, picking up the pace. The crowd are booing, they wanted Bunty's Lad to win. This will be a big turn-up for the donkeys. And here he comes into the final straight. Ol' Toney will pass the line first, and... he does! It's all over! Ol' Toney takes the donkey crown! The crowd are very upset... Oh, my, they're throwing things! Everyone's lost a *whole lot of money here and they're not happy. Wait a sec, hold your donkeys for a moment... Look! Look at the statue, everyone, it's... Sir Gossamer D'Glaze... he's collapsed. This is terrible!*

Finish

Casper and Julius surveyed the scene in horror. The rain poured down in buckets and the thunder shook the ground, while men, women, children and Lamp ran about in panic. Around the fallen statue were wailing youngsters and their agitated parents – luckily nobody was seriously hurt (apart from Sir Gossamer D'Glaze, whose pieces were strewn across the square, and who had, quite frankly, seen better days). Meanwhile, furious at losing their money through such strange circumstances, crowds of penniless villagers threw insults, punches and other villagers at the bookmaker's. Over in the far corner, little old Betty Woons was out for the count, having been hit by a speeding donkey. The local doctor was trying to bring her round with smelling salts and offers of jelly beans. At the same time Lamp had thrown off his hat and was running through the square, arms aloft, screaming something about duffel coats, and at the point where Clemmie Answorth rushed past Casper and Julius brandishing a carving knife, they knew it was time to leave.

Chapter 7

Curse on the Kobb

At this point in my tale, the whole thing gets rather weird. So if you don't like it when whole things get rather weird, I suggest you should stop reading this and do something worthwhile, like knitting, or fencing, or perhaps both at the same time. (It's called 'fenting' and is the second most dangerous sport in the world, after extreme-bear-angering.) Go on, off you pop!

Right, now they've popped off, I can carry on with my tale. To be honest, I'm glad they're gone, anyway. They were smelly and kept coughing really loudly during the good bits.

Casper awoke on Monday morning to the sound of rain. That wasn't much of a surprise – it had rained relentlessly through Saturday, got harder on Sunday and kept him awake for most of Sunday night. It was all very well having an umbrella, but with this sort of weather you really needed a boat. Some of the village had flooded: it was worst down by the village pub, The Horse and Horse, where the water was so deep you had to wear armbands. Cracklin Crescent wasn't so bad, but Casper Candlewacks had other things to worry about.

Julius hadn't got out of bed since the donkey race; he'd had enough humiliation for a lifetime, let alone a

weekend. Casper had done his best to cheer his dad up, bringing him mugs of tea and bacon sandwiches, but each time Julius just grunted and rolled over. In the end Casper gave up and spent the rest of his weekend drawing vampires and listening to the rain. He'd considered owning up about the lie; he'd even

practised what to say, but was worried about doing so while there were knives in the house.

There was a leak in the roof above the kitchen, which Casper had plugged himself (he used a banana, some masking tape and a pot of honey, and it had actually worked quite well). The TV, which had been on the blink for a while, finally gave out that morning, so Amanda was swearing at it and hitting it and threatening it with a lawsuit, but to no avail. But worst of all, Cuddles was teething. The screams could be heard from space.

There was nothing for breakfast except for a banana and some honey, but they were busy; so Casper left for school on an empty stomach. The first step outside soaked his left trainer. The second soaked his right. The third went squelch, and the rest of them did pretty much the same as the third one.

Corne-on-the-Kobb looked a state this morning: five separate angry men were struggling to get their cars started and grunting angrily every time they failed. The whole place smelt strange as well; imagine soggy cabbage mixed with barbecued socks and you're halfway there. The park was a mess; the grass had turned to sludge and the trees looked rotten and withered. Benches had blown over in the wind, as had some bushes, bits of fence and Clemmie Answorth. In her struggle to get up she'd dug herself quite a mud-pit, but Casper helped her out and offered her his coat. She shivered a "Thank you" and tottered home to dry off and warm up. By the time Casper had arrived at school, he was utterly confused. He couldn't put his finger on it; everything in the village was just… different.

The morning's lessons were terrible. Class 6 were supposed to watch a video about the Romans, but Mrs

Snagg couldn't get the TV to work. Instead, they had to copy out from their textbooks, but the pages of Casper's textbook were all stuck together and his pencil leads kept snapping. Then Lamp arrived late with an oily grin on his oily face, and even when Mrs Snagg punished his lateness with three hours' chopping wood for the staffroom fireplace, he just grinned and trotted off quite happily. Meanwhile, Anemonie Blight had pulled Teresa Louncher's hair too hard and a whole pigtail had come off in her hands. Teresa's wails were deafening. Mrs Snagg just rolled her eyes, stuck in some earplugs and got back to ogling her sizzling summer special of *Hunks in Trunks*. To top it all, Anemonie spent the rest of the morning putting clumps of hair down Casper's shirt.

Lunchtime arrived, and while the rest of the school

were allowed to stay inside, Mrs Snagg locked Class 6 out in the playground. Their spiky teacher was in plain view, sitting in the cosy staffroom, toasting marshmallows over the crackling fire and marking everyone's homework with an 'F'. Casper tried to shield himself from the monsoon, but without his coat he was soaked to the bone marrow within moments. On the other side of the playground, Anemonie had pushed Ted Treadington over into a deep puddle and was now standing on his head.

Lamp, having finished chopping his wood, spotted Casper and galloped over. "Hi! Casper!"

"Hello, Lamp," Casper sighed.

"I've got some great news!" Lamp was breathless. "Guess why I was late?"

Casper clicked his teeth. "Why?"

"I've done it! My buggy is working!" Lamp was

so excited that he did a little trot on the spot and then hiccupped.

Casper managed a doubting smile. "Well done."

"Do you want to come and try it after school?"

"I… I can't." Casper searched for an excuse. "I've got to go… fishing."

"Fishing? Can I come?"

But Casper's response was saved by a pigeon, who waddled towards Casper and cooed demandingly. Casper searched his pockets for something to feed it, and found some three-week-old stale chocolate buttons. He scattered them in the puddles in front of the pigeon, but it waded right past the buttons and carried on towards Casper.

"All right," he said, "you don't like chocolate."

Three more pigeons fluttered in to join the first, trotting towards Casper and starting to peck at his

ankles. Confused, Casper lightly kicked one away, but it just landed on Lamp's arm and started pecking that instead.

"Gerroff!" yelled Lamp, flapping his arm around.

Casper kicked more aggressively now. "Stop it. I don't have anything else!" he shouted, sending wet pigeons and clumps of feathers everywhere, but the commotion only attracted more of the blighters. Soon the whole flock was crowding around the boys, trying to get a peck of their limbs, like children round an ice-cream van, and it was really beginning to hurt.

Lamp's upper body was completely covered in pigeons now, and no shaking or screaming was going to do anything. "Help!" he shouted. "Help me!"

The rest of Class 6, who had until now thought Casper and Lamp were just playing a quick game of that family favourite, *Be Attacked by Pigeons*,

scurried over to help. But as they arrived, more pigeons launched themselves at the children and got pecking. Anemonie shrieked and tried to bat them off, but it was too late: the pigeons had already latched on to her with their little talons, unfolded their little pigeon napkins, got out their little pigeon knives and forks and tucked in. Casper shielded his face while trying desperately to shake himself free of the pigeons, but their claws dug firmly into his wet clothes and skin. Most of the class had dropped to the floor now, rolling about and screaming like terrified sausage rolls. The pigeons pecked away at Class 6 as if they were covered in the scrummiest pigeon feed this side of the bins round the back of The Boiled Sprout. Casper feared to shout for help in case a pigeon would jump inside his mouth and call it lunch; he couldn't even open his eyes for fear of pigeon-peck blindness.

He just rolled around in the puddles and wished the dirty birds would stop finding him so very tasty.

And then, suddenly – BANG!

The pigeons scattered, flying in every direction. The sixteen victims lying in the muddy puddles, exhausted and scarred, were greeted by the sight of Mayor Rattsbulge with a shotgun in hand.

"Man-pecking-pigeons, eh?" the fat mayor murmured to himself. "What next?"

Casper inspected his peck marks. He was bleeding in twelve places and his clothes were ripped. Next to him, Lamp sat half submerged in a puddle, picking feathers out of his hair. "Mayor, I… I think you just saved our lives," said Casper.

"All in a day's work, men," the portly gentleman said. Shoving his gun under one arm, he reached into his pocket, pulled out a large Cumberland sausage and took a hefty bite. He wasn't dressed in his normal mayoral attire, but in full military uniform. Far too small for his bulky frame, his bloated pink wrists and ankles poked out of his sleeves and trouser-legs, and his giant belly flopped out under his khaki shirt. (When he was younger and ate fewer pies, Mayor Rattsbulge used to be in the army. He fought in the Four Hours' War and won a medal for his animal impressions.) He put the sausage away and cleared his throat.

The class of terrified children picked themselves up and joined the mayor. Casper spoke up. "What's going on, Mr Mayor?"

"Hard to say. All started at the donkey race. Disaster after disaster." He marched up and down in front of the sixteen peckees, then he picked up his shotgun and fired straight past Casper's shoulder, hitting one stupid returning pigeon at the first attempt, producing a stinking cloud of pigeon bits and matted feathers. He continued regimentally. "This rain, the race, the statue collapsing, cars won't start, all the milk in the village has gone sour, poor Betty Woons hasn't woken up yet, not even for jelly beans…"

Ted Treadington spoke up. "My shoes didn't fit this morning, sir."

A few of the other children nodded and murmured agreement. Casper wriggled his toes in his soggy trainers. They did feel rather tight.

The mayor and his chins nodded knowingly. "Something's happening, chaps, and we've got to fight." That explained the military uniform then.

Casper frowned. "Fight who?"

"AH!" Mayor Rattsbulge's exclamation was so loud that Teresa Louncher started crying, and one

sneaky pigeon who'd almost got to Lamp (it hadn't had pudding) flapped away again in panic. "That's the question. For now, I need to get you troops inside." He ushered the bruised and shivering children of Class 6 towards the school, but as they approached the door, Mrs Snagg appeared from behind it and blocked their way with a prickly snarl.

"You're not bringing them in here, Mayor. They need their fresh air."

"Don't you dare order me about, Hillary," boomed Mayor Rattsbulge. The class giggled. "There's a war on, you know."

"I don't care if it's the end of the world, they... Oy, what are you looking at?"

 Mayor Rattsbulge was staring at Mrs Snagg's face. Casper turned to look and saw a collection of little brown lumps on her cheeks and forehead, which he was certain he'd not seen before. "Mrs Snagg, what're those things on your face?"

"There's nothing on my face, boy," she spat, reaching up to feel her skin. With horror, she traced her hands over a few little brown spots. "What… are *they*?"

Anemonie elbowed past the other children and squinted at Mrs Snagg's face. "Miss! You've got what The Great Tiramisu got!" The spots were already spreading and changing colour to a lemon yellow. Meanwhile, her face had turned lime-greenish and puffy. Anemonie cackled in Mrs Snagg's face and then skipped away, giggling.

Mrs Snagg felt the first spot burst and shrieked, "Help, make it stop!" But Mayor Rattsbulge

was distracted. He was staring at little Teresa
Louncher in revulsion, and then back to Mrs
Snagg with equal disgust.

"Your face too." He shuddered, pointing to Teresa
with a flabby finger. "You've got it as well!" He was
right; her face was covered in the little spots.

Teresa's eyes widened. She touched her cheek, felt
a spot and yelped like a puppy when you tread on its
paw. Casper watched as her face swelled too,
like a big green crying balloon with a
pigtail sticking out of one side.

"Hey," shouted Anemonie, "balloon head! I'm
gonner pop you with a pin!" And she started poking
Teresa's face, which made her cry even more.

Mrs Snagg struggled to stay on her feet
and grabbed for Mayor Rattsbulge, who
cowered away and reached for his shotgun. Teresa had

fallen to the floor again, clutching her balloon face and bawling her eyes out. Then the identical twins near the back of the group squealed and pointed at each other's spots, and Ted Treadington's face started to swell up and the rest of the class stumbled back in terror.

"Right, that's it," announced Mayor Rattsbulge, raising his shotgun and edging slowly back from the group. "Summon the troops. Call a meeting. Everyone who's not, you know, *that*, to meet in the village hall tonight at eight!" And then he turned and ran as fast as a man that size could run, screaming at the top of his voice and waving his shotgun around.

See? I told you it got weird.

Chapter 8

Laying the Blame

By eight o'clock the village hall was a buzz of excitement, like a nest of Indonesian Wasps, but with fewer wasps and less intelligence, and an awful lot more soggy idiots. Casper had convinced his dad to get out of bed and come along, but they'd left a screaming Cuddles at home with Amanda, who was taking apart the broken TV and yelling abuse at each different part. As the villagers hustled and bustled about the hall, swapping horror stories and comparing scabs, Casper willed his brain to fit the pieces together. What was happening to the village? Why was everything going all odd? And why did he feel this was his fault?

On the stage at the front of the hall was all quarter-ton of Mayor Rattsbulge, still sporting his tight-fitting military uniform, and Fatima the ferret, determinedly gnawing at her cage. The mayor had calmed down since the pigeon attack, doubtless helped by an afternoon of comfort eating (Casper noticed rather a lot of egg around his mouth and some leftover toast soldiers poking out of his top pocket). Anemonie skipped past, pointy mother in tow, and smirked poisonously at Casper and Julius.

"Yooou cursed the vill-age, yooou cursed the vill-age," she sang in her screechy little voice, and then she giggled away before Casper could respond.

Cursed? A wave of panic rushed through Casper's body. What if she was right? After all, that night in the restaurant, The Great Tiramisu did mention a curse...

The meeting was about to begin. Casper and Julius

took two seats near the back, and then Lamp trundled over, plumped himself down next to Casper and giggled.

The mayor wobbled to a standing position and surveyed the room regimentally. Some old ladies in the front row produced packed lunches from their bags and tucked in. Mayor Rattsbulge cleared his throat and began.

"People of Corne-on-the-Kobb, we have a situation."

"Situation? Ha!" mocked Audrey Snugglepuss, standing up so that everyone could see her. "This is worse than a *situation*. She scratched her head violently. "Someone's given me nits!"

"An' my courgette patch 'as been invaded by moles," said an angry Sandy Landscape, standing up to join Audrey.

"What about my front door?" squeaked a frumpy lady who, until a few hours ago, had been the proud owner of a shiny red front door. "Someone's nicked it."

"And mine."

"My teeth are falling out!"

"The buttons fell off my jacket!"

"I can't feel my legs!"

"Has anyone seen my mother?"

The place had descended into chaos. Casper felt like the pit of his stomach had tied itself in a sailor's knot. What had he done?

"SILENCE!" bellowed Mayor Rattsbulge (causing a small earthquake in Bolivia). The hall fell silent, silent as a mouse that had recently had its voice box removed. Even the old ladies were scared to chew on their sandwiches for the noise it would make.

"Now. We mustn't panic. Will everybody please remain calm?" The mayor took out his considerably shortened Cumberland sausage and took another bite, munching thoughtfully. "Right. If you wish to speak, please raise your hand."

Two hundred and four idiots raised their hands. The mayor pointed at Audrey Snugglepuss, and she began. "Isn't it obvious? We're cursed!"

A general gasp, numerous shrieks, a couple of groans and a grunt arose from the crowd. It took a good three minutes for silence to be restored. Audrey Snugglepuss scratched her head again and continued.

"Think about it – since that Great Tiramisu got poisoned, everything's been going wrong. He's cursed us."

The villagers were visibly shocked. Could it possibly be true? Murmurs of agreement (and spilt flasks of tea) trickled through the village hall. Casper crossed as many fingers as he could possibly cross and held his breath. He knew what was about to happen.

And then, what was about to happen, well, it sort of happened. Audrey Snugglepuss emitted a sudden gasp and, pointing one of her nine remaining fingers at Julius Candlewacks, she said, "…which means it's *his* fault."

Julius gulped. Every idiotic face turned round to look; expressions slipped from amusement to realisation to anger (except for Lamp's, which stayed puzzled – he didn't really understand what was happening). People began to whisper.

"Of course, it *was* him."

"He poisoned Tiramisu in the first place."

"Does he know where my mother is?"

But attention shifted again, this time back to the

stage. Fatima the ferret, who had until now been happily rooting around in her cage for tasty vole-shaped morsels, had spluttered a little ferrety sneeze. The villagers watched her with terror. Fatima sneezed again, and then sniffed, and blinked, and then sneezed rather violently, before falling neatly backwards to the floor of her cage, making a light *flump* sound and generating a little cloud of displaced straw bits that gently floated down and settled again.

Not a breath could be heard. The villagers waited for another sound out of the little ferret for a full twenty seconds. Casper grabbed his father's hand and squeezed hard. Finally, with tears in his eyes, Mayor Rattsbulge said, "Fatima… she's… *Get him!*"

Within a moment the entire village hall was screaming, crying and scrambling towards Julius Candlewacks.

"He killed Fatima!"

"Murderer!"

"He'll pay for this!"

Casper tried to shield Julius from the angry crowd, but they pushed past easily and lugged him towards the stage.

"Please, it wasn't his fault. Leave him alone!"

Julius was led towards Mayor Rattsbulge, who was clutching Fatima's floppy body to his breast and whispering into her ear. He spotted Julius and stuffed Fatima ingloriously back in her cage, wiped his eyes and straightened himself up.

"Julius Candlewacks, you've cursed our village and you've… you've killed my ferret! With the power vested in me as Mayor of Corne-on-the-Kobb, I decree that you are guilty of the utterly unforgivable crimes of curse-inducing and… um… ferret murdering; and you shall be fed to the pigeons at the strike of midnight!"

The villagers cheered savagely. Casper's mouth fell open in shock. Terror, guilt and anger pumped through his veins as he battled his way through the crowd. How could the villagers turn on his dad like this?

"You've got it *wrong*!" he cried, waving his arms around. "Julius isn't the villain, it's The Great Tiramisu. Listen to me!"

But it was useless; Mayor Rattsbulge had made his decision. "Take him away, men."

Casper couldn't believe what was happening. He caught his poor father's eye as he was dragged helplessly towards the door. "It's all my fault!" he shouted. "I'm so sorry, Dad. I'll save you, I promise!"

Julius looked back at Casper, defeat in his eyes. The villagers clapped and cheered as they carried him away, into the stormy village square. Last to leave was Anemonie Blight, sticking her slimy little tongue out at Casper and then skipping out of the door, giggling. As the door slammed shut and the hall fell silent, a big brick wall of fear hit Casper right in the face and he broke down into hot frustrated tears. He was completely alone, with no hope of saving his dad, and it was all his fault.

Casper heard a spongy shuffling noise from beside him and felt a warm arm on his shoulder. He turned to see Lamp, sporting a sympathetic smile. "Sorry, Casper. I haven't got my hanky." Casper wiped his eyes on his jumper and sobbed.

Lamp looked around the room helplessly. "Do you want a go on my buggy now?"

Chapter 9

The Bubbel Buggy

When Casper and Lamp left the village hall, it was raining so hard that if they had tried to measure it with a rain-hardness-o-meter, they would've got the reading TIME TO BUILD AN ARK. It was as heavy as Mayor Rattsbulge after Christmas dinner. It was as if a squadron of swimming-pool planes all just sprang a leak while flying over Corne-on-the-Kobb. It was like everyone in heaven had forgotten to turn off their showers and gone out for the day. Basically, it was weather for a snorkel.

As they waded back through the square, Casper looked at his chubby little companion in his greasy blue boiler suit (and saturated sponge shoes), and let out a deep sigh. Lamp Flannigan was all that he had left. He longed for his boring old life, before The Great Tiramisu, the coriander and the curse. Imaginary danger was more than enough for Casper; real-life danger was big and scary and, well, real. He wished he could rewind the tape to stop himself from taking revenge and creating this mess in the first place.

Lamp had been deep in thought for a while, and finally said, "At least in the rain no one will see you've been crying." He patted Casper on his wet back. "That's a good thing."

Casper's thoughts strayed back to Julius. "How am I going to save my dad, Lamp?"

Lamp shrugged. "Sock puppets?"

"We *need* to save him. I don't know what I'd do without him." Casper didn't want to admit it, but he knew he'd really miss his dad. Who'd wash his clothes every month? Who'd burn his dinner? Who'd change Cuddles's nappy?

Casper shuddered. "We absolutely *have* to get him back."

The boys reached what used to be the park, but was now, more accurately, a swamp. They picked their way across on the solid bits, avoiding the crocodiles.

"I've got a plan," said Lamp, "but it does involve flying and I don't think either of us can fly."

Casper was a bit behind, having almost lost his shoe to the quagmire. "We just need to lift the curse, then there'll be no need to... you know... feed the pigeons."

"But The Great Terrapin has gone, Casper, you know that," Lamp said, leaping to the next dry patch. "And I don't know how to lift any curses."

"It's my fault. I wanted to get my own back and I just got carried away. I didn't think *this* would happen." Casper caught up with Lamp on a wobbly tuffet and tipped some pond life out of his shoes.

"He deserved it," said Lamp.

"I know, but…"

"You know you can't just shout at a walrus, Casper. My mum told me that. It's bad manners."

The boys swam the rest of the way to the other side of the park and arrived exhausted, but alive. (Lamp had caught a fish in his overalls and was inspecting it hungrily.)

As hard as he'd tried, Casper still hadn't come up with a plan. "It's useless," he groaned. "I give up." He left a disappointed and muddy Lamp standing at the park gate and turned to squelch the rest of the way home, colliding head first with the postbox, still sporting the poster of The Great Tiramisu, moustache in full bloom. He grunted and trod on, before stopping in his tracks and turning back to face the poster.

"Oh, I am *such* an idiot."

"You're not really," said Lamp.

"No, look!" Casper's face was animated for the first time since the meeting. "Read the poster."

"I don't understand," said Lamp, which was true because he didn't understand. But he did as he was told and read the poster. He saw a picture of The Great Taramasalata, a little description, a list of tour dates… "I still don't understand," he said, still not understanding.

"Don't you see? The tour dates! What's today?"

"Rainy?"

"No, what day? What day is it?"

Lamp looked at his socks. "My socks say Monday."

Casper tracked his finger down the poster, mumbling to himself. "Saturday, Sunday, AH!"

"What?" The suspense was too much for Lamp's poor brain, which was fragile at the best of times. (When Lamp is asked two questions at the same time, he usually faints.)

"Upper Crustenbury! He's performing tonight in the Upper Crustenbury Village Hall!"

Lamp swapped from Casper's joyous face to the poster, and the rusty cogs in his tiny brain began to turn. "So... we go to Upper Crustybelly and find The Great Terracotta, and get him to lift the curse." Lamp clapped his hands. "Hang on, how do we do that?"

"How do I know? We'll work it out on the way."

Lamp had never been on an adventure before. "This is so exciting! I'm going to wear my glow-in-the-dark trousers."

"Please don't."

"Not the trousers. Got it."

"So it's sorted. I'll run home and get my dad to drive us to..." Casper paused. His face went pale. "Lamp... who's going to drive us there? My mum won't leave the house, and my dad's... busy."

"Well, my mum can't either. She's been banned from using any heavy machinery since that

137

tumble-drying thing last year."

Casper threw his head in his hands again. Today was by far the worst day of his life (apart from the one with the penguins, but we've covered that) and it showed no signs of getting better.

"Well," said Lamp, "we could always use my buggy."

Casper eyed Lamp with pity. "Look, Lamp. Your inventions don't work. They've never worked. You can't run an engine on washing-up liquid."

"But I have! I've made it work!"

"You haven't!" Casper was soaked and upset and still not in the mood for Lamp's make-believe machines. "You can't have."

Lamp fixed Casper in the eye and spoke very slowly. "Casper, I know you think I'm stupid. I probably am. I mess up my words and I fall over, and

I can't do my times tables or read books like you can. But you have to believe me, Casper. My buggy works, and I *can* drive us to Upper Crustybelly, and we *can* save your dad."

"I… I'm sorry, Lamp." Casper closed his eyes. "I didn't mean to be rude."

"It's OK. Now, come on, what are we waiting for?"

Casper nodded his head. He might as well give it a try; it wasn't as if he had any other options. Lamp's buggy, however absurd, was his only chance to save his dad.

"All right then, let's go."

As they hurried off together towards Lamp's house, Lamp tripped over his own feet and sloshed to the ground.

Five soaking minutes and twenty-three soggy seconds later, the two boys had arrived. Lamp's garage was a place of wonder. Spanners, wrenches and pencil sharpeners of all shapes and sizes hung on the walls. Spare wheels and planks of wood were piled up in the corner by an old transistor radio wired up to a microwave. "When there's salsa music playing, it makes the food hot," he explained.

Just above that a hamster was running furiously on a wheel, barely powering the dim light bulb that illuminated the garage. The whole place smelt of burning and soap. To Casper's right was a large blackboard, covered in Lamp's complicated chalky scribblings, like

$$Spede = (\sqrt{Bubbels} \times Acselarashun)^2$$

and

$$Critikal\ Mass = \pi \div Numbar\ of\ Weels$$

But taking up most of the space was Lamp's washing-up-liquid-powered buggy. Casper stared at the vehicle in awe. Lamp's mum's two-seater leather sofa sat within a sturdy metal frame, supported by four wonky tractor wheels. On the driver's side was a wooden steering wheel made from a toilet seat, and a bent golf club for a gear stick. To finish it off, Lamp had written THE BUBBEL BUGGY down each side in

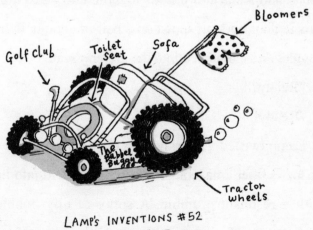

Golf club

Toilet Seat

Sofa

Bloomers

The Bubbel Buggy

Tractor wheels

LAMP'S INVENTIONS #52
The Bubbel Buggy

vibrant pink paint and attached a pair of his mum's bloomers to a broomstick on the top of the frame for a makeshift flag.

"Lamp, this is… incredible."

"Do you like it?"

"I'll like it if it drives us to Upper Crustenbury."

Lamp chuckled and nodded for Casper to climb in. It was surprisingly comfortable, actually (once Casper had found a place to put his legs). Lamp yanked the garage door open, snapped on a pair of antique flying goggles and clambered into the driver's seat.

"Ready?"

"Ready!"

Lamp twisted a doorknob on the dashboard and to Casper's utter amazement the engine kicked into life with a resonant grumble. A spray of oily bubbles spewed from the exhaust pipe on to the garage floor,

and with a grind of the
golf club they were off.
Casper roared with delight as
they turned the corner and
splashed down the flooded
street, causing a minor tidal
wave that destroyed Sandy

Landscape's cabbages. Within moments they were
speeding away from the village, off to find The Great
Tiramisu, and save Casper's dad.

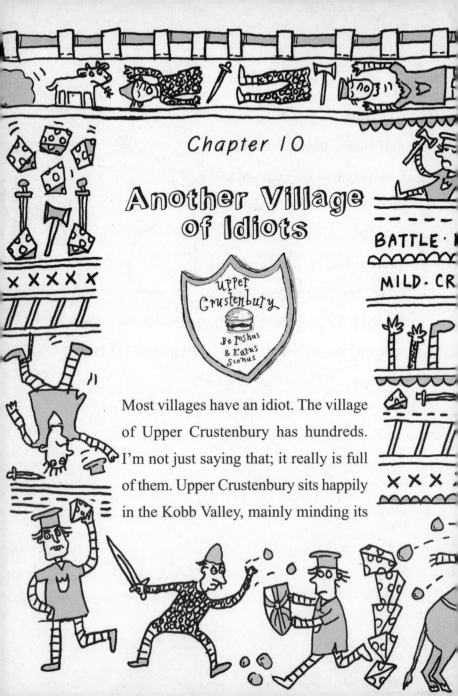

Chapter 10

Another Village of Idiots

Upper Crustenbury

Be Poshus & Eatus Sconus

Most villages have an idiot. The village of Upper Crustenbury has hundreds. I'm not just saying that; it really is full of them. Upper Crustenbury sits happily in the Kobb Valley, mainly minding its

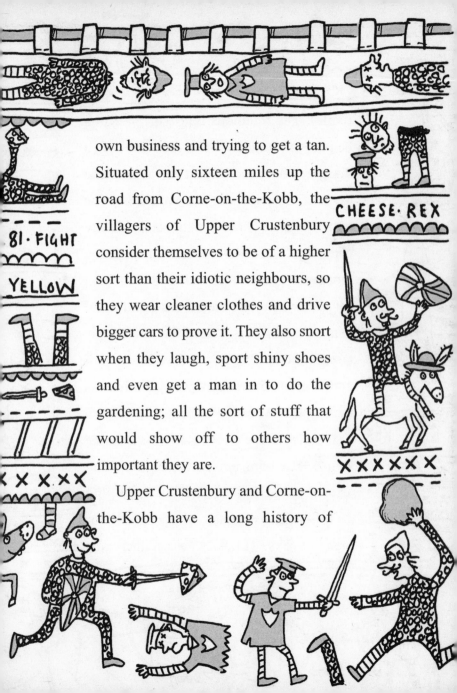

own business and trying to get a tan. Situated only sixteen miles up the road from Corne-on-the-Kobb, the villagers of Upper Crustenbury consider themselves to be of a higher sort than their idiotic neighbours, so they wear cleaner clothes and drive bigger cars to prove it. They also snort when they laugh, sport shiny shoes and even get a man in to do the gardening; all the sort of stuff that would show off to others how important they are.

Upper Crustenbury and Corne-on-the-Kobb have a long history of

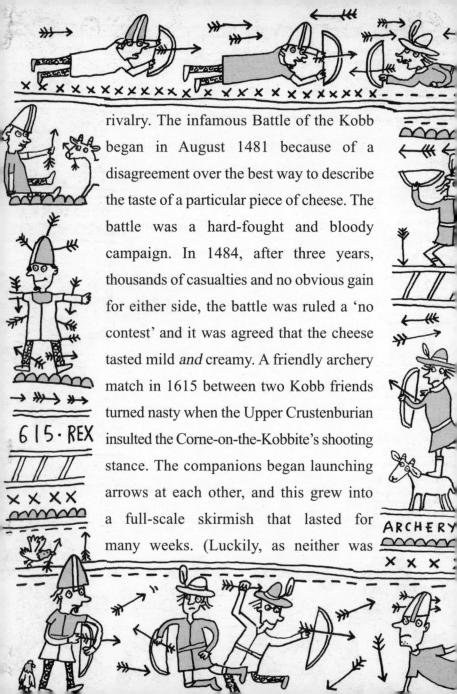

rivalry. The infamous Battle of the Kobb began in August 1481 because of a disagreement over the best way to describe the taste of a particular piece of cheese. The battle was a hard-fought and bloody campaign. In 1484, after three years, thousands of casualties and no obvious gain for either side, the battle was ruled a 'no contest' and it was agreed that the cheese tasted mild *and* creamy. A friendly archery match in 1615 between two Kobb friends turned nasty when the Upper Crustenburian insulted the Corne-on-the-Kobbite's shooting stance. The companions began launching arrows at each other, and this grew into a full-scale skirmish that lasted for many weeks. (Luckily, as neither was

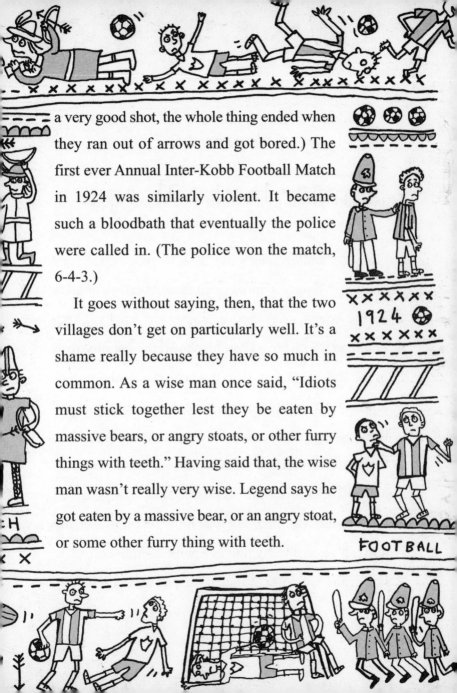

a very good shot, the whole thing ended when they ran out of arrows and got bored.) The first ever Annual Inter-Kobb Football Match in 1924 was similarly violent. It became such a bloodbath that eventually the police were called in. (The police won the match, 6-4-3.)

It goes without saying, then, that the two villages don't get on particularly well. It's a shame really because they have so much in common. As a wise man once said, "Idiots must stick together lest they be eaten by massive bears, or angry stoats, or other furry things with teeth." Having said that, the wise man wasn't really very wise. Legend says he got eaten by a massive bear, or an angry stoat, or some other furry thing with teeth.

Chapter 10.1

Murder in the Marquee

Casper Candlewacks's day was getting better very quickly. Very, very quickly, in fact. About as quickly as the speed of a certain buggy driven by Lamp Flannigan. The boys scorched down the country road in the Bubbel Buggy (leaving behind a frothy trail of lemon-fresh bubble exhaust), howling with joy, the thrill of the ride leaving no free space in their little brains to worry about what lay ahead. As soon as they had left Corne-on-the-Kobb the rain had subsided and the late evening sun was now peeping over the horizon like a cheeky lion in a game of hide-and-seek. For a few welcome minutes Casper was completely distracted from the scrunching worry that languished at the pit of his stomach like a chunk of unchewed pork chop. To top it all, he didn't even have to wear a seatbelt. (Even if he had wanted to wear a seatbelt he couldn't have because Lamp had forgotten to attach any. There were, however, holders for ice-cream cones in case they stopped for one, so that was OK.)

Casper whooped and punched the air. He was boy adventurer Casper Candlewacks, saving the world once more with his sidekick, gadget-man Lamp Flannigan. "We need superhero outfits," shouted Casper.

"Can mine glow in the dark?" said Lamp.

"Course it can."

The road broadened into a quiet street, leading into the centre of Upper Crustenbury.

"Ahh, look at that sunset," said Lamp, leaning back into the comfy leather sofa, hands behind his head.

"Lamp! Watch the road!"

Lamp looked down, yelped and swerved wildly to the right, only just avoiding a small hedgehog that was fast asleep on the sun-warmed tarmac and dreaming of crunchy beetles. But his steering had driven the boys off the road and right through a tidy little front lawn. Casper screamed as the Bubbel Buggy veered left again, back on to the road and straight off again on the other side, crushing another front garden and destroying a quaint little community of garden gnomes.

"Use the brakes!" Casper shouted.

"I can't! There aren't any!"

They clattered through a wooden fence, shooting splintered planks and flecks of mud in every direction. Lamp grappled with the toilet seat and swung to the right, but he steered too far and the Bubbel Buggy twisted back on itself and tore up the same garden, squashing any gnomes that had escaped the first salvo.

Dodging a garden shed, the boys ploughed through a washing line full of clothes, and Lamp found himself tangled up in a rather fetching pair of woollen tights (which, incidentally, were just his size). Casper screamed as the Bubbel Buggy careered up a grassy slope and down the other side, almost flipping itself over. It cannoned through another fence and on to a wide village green, heading directly for a large white marquee in the centre. Casper grabbed the toilet seat and spun it to the left, but it came straight off in his hands.

"Lamp! The steering wheel!"

Lamp was still struggling with the tights.

Casper looked in terror from the toilet seat in his hands to the oncoming marquee. "I can't steer!"

The Bubbel Buggy piled head-on into the marquee, ripping through the canvas and coming to an abrupt halt inside.

"Let's park here," said Lamp. He spotted the detached toilet seat in Casper's hand and tutted loudly. "That's where it is!" he said, and slotted it back on its axle.

Casper exhaled and let his head drop, relieved that he was in one piece and not sloshed around the village like an exploded jar of pasta sauce.

The boys shakily alighted from their battered

buggy and fell to the ground, exhausted. Casper raised his eyes for the first time and noticed their strange surroundings. The marquee had been set out as if for a party, with long lines of trestle tables covered by green paper tablecloths. Green plates and cups marked out the places, and every so often along the tables was a large glass bottle of green liquid. The marquee itself had been adorned with huge garlands of leafy herbs, and even more herbs had been strewn on the ground to make a sort of forest floor. Around the edges were sculptures of historical figures, constructed entirely out of herbs. There was Herb Napoleon, Herb Winston Churchill and the full line-up of Herby Spice Girls. A stage had been constructed (out of herbs) at the end of the marquee and it too was covered in herbs – buckets of the stuff in fact. Centre stage there was a herby jacket that was hung up on a herby hanger right next to a massive herby hat. Behind that, at the back of the stage, sat a bath, filled to the brim with a great big heap of herbs (for a change). The whole place had a familiar, fragrant smell that Casper just couldn't place.

Lamp was munching on some floor-herbs. "Mm," he slopped, "what ish thish shtuff?"

"Come on, Lamp," said Casper, picking himself up from the floor. "We *have* to get to The Great Tiramisu before he leaves the village."

"But we haven't had dinner, and it's…" Lamp looked at his watch and frowned, "it's dinnertime."

"Not now. Come on!" Casper raced away, dragging Lamp begrudgingly behind him. Lamp managed to stuff a handful of floor-herbs into his pocket before Casper could pull him out of the marquee and off in search of The Great Tiramisu.

Alone in the marquee, the washing-up liquid

engine of the Bubbel Buggy ticked over obediently and a little plume of bubbles spewed out of the exhaust pipe, adding to the ever-growing pile of soapy froth that was building up behind the back wheels. The pile grew and grew, as more and more foam coughed out of the back of the little buggy…

"Where are those hoodlums going in such a blithering hurry?" asked a disgruntled Lord Quentin de Llanbarton-Smithe, as two raggedy boys hurtled past the gravel drive of his semi-detached mansion, in which he currently sat with his wife, Lady Gwynette de Llanbarton-Smithe, enjoying a spot of supper. Like every meal eaten by the upper classes, tonight's menu was tea and scones. Lord and Lady de Llanbarton-Smithe were not born into the aristocracy; in order to fit in with all the other lords and ladies in Upper Crustenbury they bought their titles off the Internet.

LORD & LADY de LLANBARTON-SMITHE

"Himph!" Lady Gwynette snorted. "It's a positive miracle I didn't spill my tea, what with all those ruffians making all that racket. Himph!" She put down her tea and sniffed the air with disgust. "Oh, my, and the *smell* of them," she said, and covered her nose with her lavender-scented handkerchief.

Lord Quentin nodded sagely. "Fetid, my dear, quite fetid." He took a measured bite of his jam-laden scone.

"Delinquents like that shouldn't be allowed, not in this day and age."

"I blame the government," said Lady Gwynette, scowling. "It's a positive outrage." She shook her head, sipped her tea and concluded, "Himph!"

"Another scone, darling?"

"Oh, but Quenty, I positively mustn't," warbled Lady Gwynette. She eyed the plate of cakes hungrily. "Oh, all right, you jolly well forced my arm. I shall just have a teensy little one," and she took the largest, jammiest scone on the plate.

Chapter 11

Telling Tiramisu

As the last of the sun disappeared below the horizon, the boys sprinted towards the village hall, soapy feet pounding on the cobbled streets (which is good because the cobbled streets needed a good wash, actually). "Come on, Lamp!" called Casper, stopping for a moment to catch his breath and to let his chubby companion catch up.

Lamp lumbered towards Casper, gasping for air and sweating like a chipmunk in an oven. He wasn't too good at running. He wasn't even particularly good at walking. (He'd never tried skipping, but he doubted he'd be much better at that.) "Sorry, Casper." He slowed to a stop and leant on a wall. "It's my asthma."

"Lamp, you don't have asthma."

"Then it's my eczema."

"But eczema doesn't do that!"

"Mine does."

Casper shook his head. "Look, it doesn't matter. We have to go!" He fought the aching in his legs and set off down the next street and on to the cobbled village square, with Lamp panting away not far behind. Spotting the village hall at the other corner, Casper was horrified to see the final trickle of haughty Upper Crustenburians trotting out of the doors, honking away about "The Great Tiramisu's spiffing wand action". The show had ended, but The Great Tiramisu was nowhere to be seen.

"Quick, Lamp, we might be too late." Casper ran over to an elderly woman standing by the village hall, who looked like a wrinkly horse with a tweed suit and jodhpurs, while Lamp staggered on behind.

"Excuse me, miss…"

The woman flared her gigantic nostrils. "What ho, chappies!"

Casper noticed that her shoes didn't match. "Can you tell us where to find The Great Tiramisu?"

"Where've you been? On the jolly moon?" She threw her head back and guffawed. "He's gorn to the marquee for the coriander festival."

"The *what*?" Casper's heart did a backflip.

"Coriander, Casper," explained Lamp. He reached into his pocket and pulled out some of the floor-herbs. "This stuff."

Casper took a pinch and sniffed it. That familiar scent filled his nostrils again, and as it wafted through the air a memory jarred in Casper's brain like a tone-deaf cat jumping on a piano. "Coriander…"

Lamp guzzled a massive mouthful and chewed gratefully. "Ichh ruvvry."

"No, Lamp, it's *coriander*!"

He still wasn't getting it.

"Look, swallow your herbs and listen to me."

Lamp did as he was told (it took about four gulps – it was a very large mouthful) and smiled at Casper.

"Right, The Great Tiramisu is about to step inside a marquee filled with coriander. There's enough inside there to make his head explode…"

Casper thought he could hear a slow clicking noise in Lamp's head, followed by something like the clang of a ship's bell. Lamp shuffled backwards, struck by the news. "…and if he doesn't have a head, he won't be able to lift the curse!"

"There's only one thing for it," said Casper determinedly. "We run again, now!"

"Oh, no," groaned Lamp. "More running." He trundled off after Casper, who was already halfway back across the square.

"Pip pip!" shouted the tweedy woman, waving heartily, and then she cantered off home to chomp on a sugar cube.

Back raced the two heroes, over the cobbled streets,

past the gravel drives and perfectly trimmed hedges;
the greatest double act since Batman and Robin, Butch
and Sundance, Kylie and Jason, Bill and Ben…

Purple-faced and puffing like a blueberry smoking
a pipe, Lamp slowed to a halt and grabbed his
stomach. "I… can't… go on…"

"It's fine," said Casper. "It's just round this corner."
They staggered the few final steps to the end of the
street, but as they glimpsed the village green, lit by
hundreds of herby lanterns, Casper's heart sank. They
were greeted with the belly-wrenching sight of the
amassed gaggle of snooty Upper-Crustenburians
gathering at the entrance to the marquee, bustling
about, babbling to each other in high-pitched whinnies
and shooing away the upper-class pigeons that had
come for a spot of supper. They were headed by a
staggeringly posh mayor and the evil curse-caster

himself, The Great Tiramisu, ever-resplendent moustache glistening in the lantern-light like a well-groomed toilet brush. He smiled regally and outstretched his arms, knocking over a little boy asking for his autograph.

Lord Octavius Wimperly-Fescott the Third (Mayor of Upper Crustenbury, Marquis of Leith and Owner of Money) clasped his hands together and briskly cleared his throat. He spoke in a series of nasal squawks and hoots, with such an impeccably posh accent that it would have made the royal family sound common.

"Ahem. Most distinguished guests, Dukes and Duchesses, Barons and Baronesses, Viscounts and—"

"Thank you, thank you. You are-a too kind." The Great Tiramisu barged Mayor Wimperly-Fescott out of the way with a well-placed elbow jab. "You are-a most honoured to have-a me here. My performance was, I think you will agree, *magnifico*."

The crowd responded with hoots of approval; an eager chap at the front with a waistcoat and far too many teeth, proclaimed, "Hear hear!"

"And now," continued the mayor, who was so posh that he wore two bow ties, "it gives me the utmost gratification to bequeath upon you a little surprise." He waltzed towards the opening of the marquee.

"STOP! Don't open up that marquee," came a shout from the back of the crowd. The villagers screeched with confusion and whisked around to see a small, scruffy, blond-haired boy frantically pushing his way through the mob, smelling of lemon and rather red in the face. Following behind him was his equally fragrant companion, sporting a boiler suit and clutching his ribs.

Casper spoke up again. "You mustn't open it up!

Tiramisu, listen to me, it'll kill you." The crowd was aghast; many of the ladies screamed theatrically and fell into their husbands' arms. One lady, who forgot that she didn't have a husband, fell flat on her back.

Mayor Wimperly-Fescott was about as happy as a puppy with a paper cut. His chest swelled, his lips pursed. "I do beg your blithering pardon?"

"*Si*," said The Great Tiramisu. "What you mean, 'kill-a me'?"

"I mean just that," said Casper. "What's in that marquee – it'll kill you. I beg you, please don't go in there." More gasps arose from the villagers.

"You!" The Great Tiramisu bristled his moustache. "You are the dirty *bambini* from Corne-on-the-Kobb."

With idiotic eyebrows raised, the villagers began to whisper. The whispers gradually built into murmurs and the murmurs grew into angry yells.

"Corne-on-the-Kobb? Poor show."

"How very coarse; why are *they* here?"

"Those ragamuffins are trying to ruin our festival."

"I say we jolly well throw them out."

"They need a good flogging, I'll warrant."

"Tar-and-feather them!"

"Chop orf their heads!"

Two young men with floppy hair and wellies stepped forward and grabbed hold of Casper and Lamp by the scruff of their necks with vice-like neck-scruff grips. They dragged them out of the back of the crowd and dropped them coldly to the grass. Exhausted and defeated, the boys didn't get up.

"We've lost, Lamp." Casper looked at his friend emptily. "They're not going to listen to us. After all we've done, we've still lost."

"Hang on," said Lamp, rooting around in the grass.

"I'll see if I can find a four-leafed clover. That'll sort things out."

Casper slammed his fist to the ground in anger. "It's not fair! We could've saved my dad, but now he's pigeon feed and it's all my fault!" Casper held his head in his hands and pressed his eyes shut, trying with every speck of his remaining energy not to cry, but the tears forced themselves through. He imagined his father being led towards the pigeon cage, looking out for his beloved son, waiting for some heroic plan that would save the day. He imagined the looks on the faces of the idiotic villagers, whooping madly at every pigeon peck. He imagined the future – having to get a job, pay the bills and look after Amanda and Cuddles. It was all over now. Casper was scared, crushed and alone.

Lamp hadn't found a four-leafed clover. He had, however, found a stag beetle, and was poking it with a twig, which he'd also found.

"And now, oh Great Tiramisu," announced Mayor Wimperly-Fescott, tooting tunefully, "without further intrusion, I shall continue. We, the hallowed residents of Upper Crustenbury, welcome you as distinguished guest of honour at our wondrous festival of…" and with a flourish the mayor ripped open the marquee's awning. Instantly a dense wall of soapy froth flopped out of the entrance, on to the grass at his feet. "…of… bubbles?"

Chapter 12

Bubbles?

Everybody was silent, silent as a whole group of mice that had just discovered that two little mice from another mouse hole had ruined their annual cheese festival.

The mayor, bow ties a-quiver, broke the silence. "… Bubbles?"

Some of the crowd murmured to their neighbours, "Bubbles?"

Lamp and Casper's eyes met. Casper blinked and shook his head. "Bubbles?"

Then attention shifted to The Great Tiramisu, whose eyes had not moved from the thick plume of washing-up froth still piling out of the marquee. He raised his eyes from the bubbles to the mayor and then to the shocked crowd. His moustache twitched and then he opened his mouth to speak.

"BUBBLES!" he sang in pure delight, and he bounded gaily towards the soapy mass. He dived in, sending clumps of foam flying in all directions, covering the mayor and the front of the crowd from head to toe. He frolicked away like a piglet in a sludge pit, clutching handfuls of froth and blowing them into the air and squealing with joy again as he dived back in. Re-emerging with a grin on his face the size of Mayor Wimperly-Fescott's bank statements, he sang, "I love-a the bubbles!"

The villagers looked at one another, wide-eyed. Where had their blinking coriander festival gone? What the blazes was that Great Tiramisu doing? And

most importantly, how long
until blithering suppertime?

As the Upper Crustenburians looked on agape at The Great Tiramisu leaping about in his ever-growing bubblebath, Lamp leant over to Casper with a knowing wink. "I think I know what happened."

Casper also had a theory. "The Buggy?"

"Yeah! I left the engine running."

"And all the coriander is buried beneath the bubbles!"

"Did I just save The Great Tentacle's life?"

"I think you did, Lamp. You're a genius."

Lamp chuckled and rearranged his boiler suit. "I know."

But while The Great Tiramisu was having the time of his life in his bubbly paradise, Mayor Wimperly-Fescott was not amused. In fact, to say he was a bit on the angry side would be like saying Mayor Rattsbulge was a bit on the podgy side. The mayor's face trembled, his white lips were pursed; his Adam's apple had swollen to the size of a scotch egg, putting worrying amounts of pressure on his bow ties. "Who is behind this japery?" he demanded.

"Hi! Over here," called out Lamp, lifting himself clumsily to his feet.

The crowd gasped.

"Bring them here!" yelled the mayor.

Meanwhile The Great Tiramisu had moulded an elegant foamy beard and oversized bubble eyebrows, and was now displaying them to the crowd. "You look-a to me, I make-a the bubble face!" he said, but for the first time in his life, no one was watching him. The mayor's irate face had bulged and flushed like a knobbly potato, and as Casper and Lamp approached they could see his whole frame wobbling with swallowed rage. He scowled at the two boys as if they

177

had been bathing in cowpats, or spending his money, or any number of other disgusting things.

"Can you guttersnipes quite fathom what you've accomplished?" he spat.

"Yes, sir," they said together. Lamp giggled.

"And you consider it amusing?"

"Yes, sir."

If looks could bake cakes, Mayor Wimperly-Fescott's furious leer would've rustled up a triple-layered, poison-flavoured, exploding gateau with full-fat frog spawn icing, topped with a sprinkling of crushed scorpion tails and mouse droppings. (One of his

bow ties, unable to take the pressure, pinged away and hit the toothy chap from the front row on the nose.) "Why, you oafs, you snivelling urchins, you—"

"EEK!"

All eyes swung to The Great Tiramisu, suddenly frozen in the bubbles and staring in terror at a little speck of green floating in the froth. For a moment he remained still, and then he spotted another green speck and another. His face curled up into a deathly grimace, his still-bubbly eyebrows bending and skewing like caterpillars at a party, his perfectly white teeth beginning to chatter in his trembling mouth.

"C-C-CORIANDER!" he shrieked. He was surrounded by it; the little green specks of pure evil had formed a perfect circle round the magician and were advancing slowly upwards as more bubbles surged out of the marquee. The Great Tiramisu's arms shot out from the killer froth and above his head, and he twisted around, searching for an escape. "Help! Help-a me!" he cried. "The coriander! My beautiful face cannot take any more!"

The poor villagers hadn't a clue what was happening. They muttered to each other that perhaps it was the start of a magic trick, or a piece of modern dance, or something that Italian people just like to do. The toothy chap had other ideas and tried to throw The Great Tiramisu a mint.

"No, you *idiota*!" The coriander had crept above his waist now. "Get me out! Save-a me!"

The toothy chap shrugged and offered the rest of his mints to the villagers, who hooted with delight and helped themselves.

Casper had been standing back, watching the scene

unfold, but at that moment he was struck by a very clever, and very heroic, plan. His plan was so clever and so heroic, in fact, that Hercules's older, more heroic and much cleverer brother, Heroicles, who had done *thirteen* labours and had won the latest series of *Greece's Brainiest Hero* without even doing any revision, would have taken one look at Casper and retired a broken man. Casper grabbed Lamp and stepped towards the bubble bath.

"Hello, Mr Tiramisu," he said as calmly as he could.

The Great Tiramisu, shaking violently and sweating like a Brazilian woolly-jumper salesman, cried, "You, boys, please-a get me out! The coriander is all around-a me! Please-a help!"

"Yes, we'll help you," said Casper, staying where he was.

"Quick! The coriander is-a coming!" It was still rising and had reached The Great Tiramisu's chest. "I'm too young and handsome to die…"

"We'll help you, but only if you make us a promise."

"Yes, anything. I-a promise anything. Just GET ME OUT!"

Casper crossed his fingers. "Lift the curse that you placed on Corne-on-the-Kobb."

"All right! I will lift-a the curse!"

182

"And stop being so mean to your animals," added Lamp.

He looked down at the coriander, creeping ever closer towards him. "OK, I promise, I promise! Anything to save my poor-a sweet face."

"And stop treating everyone like we're your servants," said Casper.

"Yes! I promise! You are-a good people, I am sorry!"

"Do you swear you'll do those things?"

"I swear! Now save-a me!"

"Do you swear on your moustache?"

The coriander had reached The Great Tiramisu's shoulders. He yelped in fear and grasped his beloved quivering moustache. "I swear, I swear! Anything! Please!" Then the first speck of coriander touched his neck – he screamed and collapsed, crumpling down deep under the sea of bubbles, well and truly lost in its soapy depths.

"Oh, Casper," cried Lamp, "what do we do now?"

Casper shut his eyes, took a deep breath, and dived in.

Chapter 13

Under the Bubbles

Casper swam through the herb-infested bubbles in search of The Great Tiramisu. He took an accidental gulp of the lemon-fresh foam, which stung the back of his throat as it went down. Not daring to open his eyes, he floundered about blindly in the dark, hoping to grab The Great Tiramisu's arm, leg, or moustache, but none of them were anywhere to be found. Lungs bursting, Casper came up for air.

"I can't find him!" he called to Lamp.

Behind Lamp stood the snooty villagers, sucking their mints and watching intently, but still rather confused. Then a tall woman in a bonnet choked on her mint and pointed to Casper's right, screeching, "There he is!"

Casper saw a head appear above the surface, gasp for breath and then submerge again. He leapt towards it, but by the time he got there The Great Tiramisu had disappeared.

"No, over there!" shouted a red-faced jolly fellow, getting the idea.

Casper caught sight of a moustache and dived to the left this time, but once more there was nothing. Emerging again, he saw every snooty villager pointing in a different direction, squealing and hopping about.

"It's no use," Casper shouted, "we need to get rid of these bubbles!"

"Hmm," thought Lamp. Thinking was difficult for Lamp at the best of times; he scrunched up his eyes and scratched his head and stuck out his tongue, and

he begged his brain to think of something useful for a change. After a few seconds, he clicked his fingers and grinned. "Put the buggy in reverse."

Casper, struggling to stay afloat, frowned. "What?"

"Trust me, Casper, just do it."

There was no time for discussion. Casper launched himself towards the buggy with his best doggy paddle. He could see Lamp's mum's bloomers flapping gloriously on their broomstick, high above the bubbles. With the tide of bubbles against him, every stroke was exhausting, but his dad's life depended on it, he told himself. Time to be a hero.

Eyes and throat stinging, legs in agony, lungs bursting, Casper flung forward an arm and felt cold metal. With the last of his energy he clasped the golf club and jerked it away from him into reverse. The engine choked and wheezed like a lawn mower with asthma and then broke into a broad whooshing sound as the exhaust pipe began to suck the bubbles back in. Within moments, huge billows of foam were swarming towards him and back into the engine, like a swarm of Indonesian Engineering Wasps keen to examine the inside of an exhaust pipe.

"It sucks them back in!" Casper clapped his hands. "It's working!"

As the bubbles flushed away, he was able to see Lamp hopping about nervously outside the marquee, searching the shallows for The Great Tiramisu. Then at last he stopped, pointed, and shouted, "Casper, I've found him!"

All Casper wanted was a massage and a lie-down, but with the bubbles now at his ankles, he sprinted back out towards Lamp. As he left the marquee he could clearly see The Great Tiramisu outside, lying motionless on the floor, covered in green-speckled soapy bubble remains.

Casper rushed over. "Quick, get these clothes off him. He can't be near any coriander."

Needing no more encouragement, the women of the village (who found The Great Tiramisu rather dishy) squealed and ripped off his trousers and cape and began to bicker over who most deserved them. It was quickly agreed that one lady, who had produced a sharp little hat pin from her bonnet, was entitled to both.

"I think he's dead," said Lamp, as he watched The Great Tiramisu. He lay still, dressed only in a pair of shiny purple underpants, a purple jacket and a purple top hat, his tongue lolling out of his mouth like a lazy slug.

Mayor Wimperly-Fescott bustled through the crowd, face knobbly as ever and steaming with anger, both bow ties now removed to make space for his trembling Adam's apple. "Look what you've done," he honked. "You've topped our blithering guest!" He strode towards the boys, fists clenched, but as he approached, Casper snatched The Great Tiramisu's wrist and felt for a pulse.

"No, sir, he's alive. He's just passed out from all that coriander *you* poisoned him with."

"What? I… poisoned…" The mayor stuttered and stood back, stunned. It was his fault? But that would mean paying compensation, and that would mean giving away his money, and that would mean less money to roll around in… Mayor Wimperly-Fescott shuddered and stumbled back into the crowd.

Casper turned once again to the matter in hand. "Hey, Mr Tiramisu," he shouted, "wake up!"

The Great Tiramisu didn't stir.

"Wakey wakey," Lamp joined in, shaking The Great Tiramisu's arm, "rise and shine, breakfast time!"

Still nothing.

"Maybe he's not hungry," said Lamp.

The Great Tiramisu looked peaceful lying there, but time was running out and the curse hadn't been lifted.

"How about smelling salts?" said Casper. "Strong smells are meant to bring people round."

"Smelly…" Lamp looked frantically around himself. "Ooh, I know!" He kicked off his left shoe, unpeeled his Monday sock and waved it in front of The Great Tiramisu's nose. Nothing happened. Lamp shrugged, pulled open The Great Tiramisu's mouth, and stuffed the sock inside.

Instantly The Great Tiramisu spluttered, choked and awoke, coughing the sock and a lungful of bubbles out on to the ground beside him, before gasping for fresh air. He took a few moments to work out who he was, and then saw the chaotic scene around him, the boys standing over him, the snooty villagers and his skinny exposed legs and purple pants. Slowly, he murmured, "I… look… *ridicolo…*"

"Uh-oh…" whispered Lamp.

But then something very mysterious happened; something about as mysterious as a UFO taking the Loch Ness monster on a mysterious trip to the moon and having a chat on the way about something very mysterious. All of the silliness that surrounded The Great Tiramisu – the sea of bubbles, the coriander festival, the village of idiots, his purple top hat and purple Y-fronts glinting in the candlelight; well, if someone is surrounded by so much silliness, they can't help but absorb some of it. So it makes sense that The Great Tiramisu, lying there all exposed on the floor, began to titter.

Casper blinked and turned to Lamp. "Why is he…?"

Lamp shrugged.

The Great Tiramisu's titter grew into a chuckle. "I… I look… *ridicolo*!" He looked down at himself again and cackled, slapping his pale thigh and cackling again.

Lamp had begun to chuckle too. Casper was holding back a grin.

The Great Tiramisu had tears in his eyes as he rolled about on the grass in fits of giggles. "Look at-a me! Look at-a me!" he cried, pointing to his half-naked frame and guffawing. "I look *ridicolo*!"

Casper was laughing too now, Lamp was in stitches, and even the villagers chortled away (although they had absolutely no idea what was funny).

The Great Tiramisu held his
stomach and rocked back and
forth, Casper had to lean on
Lamp to keep himself
upright, and Lamp
had given himself
hiccups.

The children laughed and the upper-class pigeons laughed and the little sleeping hedgehog laughed; everyone laughed until their stomachs ached and their funny bones ran out of laughing juice.

"You boys," guffawed The Great Tiramisu, clambering to his feet. "You boys-a saved my life! With bubbles!" He tipped his head back and laughed again. "You beautiful *bambini*!" and with a squeal of delight he skipped over to the two boys and embraced them, kissing their foreheads one after another, squealing again and ruffling their hair. All of the Upper Crustenburians broke into a round of rapturous applause (apart from Mayor Wimperly-Fescott, that is, who crossed his arms resentfully and longed to go home and count his money).

"Huzzah!" shouted the toothy fellow at the front.

"Bravo!" another chap called.

"Encore!" added a third.

Lamp, still hiccupping, spat on his hand and rubbed the kisses off his forehead. Casper grinned and waved to the crowd.

When the crowd's cheering died down and The Great Tiramisu had got bored of cuddling his saviours, Casper said, "Mr Tiramisu, you made us a promise and we don't have much time left. The villagers are feeding my dad to the pigeons at midnight."

A handful of the villagers (and a nearby pigeon) chuckled at the absurd claim.

"No!" The Great Tiramisu called to the crowd. "Is not-a funny." He looked gravely at Casper and Lamp. "Killer pigeons never funny." He took out his wand and twirled it around, and it made a little *ding!* noise, a bit like a microwave when it's finished cooking your turnips. "There," he said, "it is done!"

Casper had never felt so relieved. He grinned and shook The Great Tiramisu's hand a little too vigorously. Lamp clapped and wiggled about with joy, and the villagers cheered and threw their top hats or children in the air, depending on which was worth less money.

"You'll not regret this!" said Casper.

"But you *bambini* be quick," The Great Tiramisu said. "The curse, it still takes time to wear off. The pigeons they still eat-a your papa."

"What?" said Casper, shocked. He turned to Lamp. "We have to get back and set Dad free! Come on!"

The Great Tiramisu, Mayor Wimperly-Fescott and the gathered Upper Crustenburians watched as Casper grabbed Lamp's arm and disappeared off inside the marquee. There was a whole minute of silence, followed by the chugging into gear of an engine. Then, with a roar, the Bubbel Buggy ripped right through the canvas of the marquee, spraying a bubbly mess in every direction, Lamp and Casper perched triumphantly on top. They took one precarious lap round the marquee (with Lamp's mum's bloomers flapping triumphantly in the wind) and then belched off towards the road, leaving clouds of soapy spume filling the air. The ruined marquee teetered for a few moments, and then with surprising grace, it collapsed, deflating on top of itself and crushing the contents of the doomed coriander festival.

As the lords and ladies filed away, honking and cheering and snorting vigorously, the children of the village larked about in the frothy trail of bubble exhaust, building bubble castles and playing bubble tag, and doing all of the other things children normally do when they find a field full of bubbles.

"Positively terrific, wasn't it, Quenty?" Lady Gwynette tittered as she strolled away from the village green, arm in arm with Lord Quentin, and she broke into a gleeful skip. "All those bubbles and the marquee and those *spiffing* boys! It was positively fabulous!"

"Blithering waste of coriander, if you ask me," grumbled Lord Quentin, wiping the last of the foam off his tailored suit.

"Well, I thought it was jolly fantastic, and I shan't hear another word of it!" Lady Gwynette said, concluding with a razor-sharp, "Himph!"

Chapter 14

The Broken Buggy

"Faster!" shouted Casper, as the Bubbel Buggy spluttered shakily round a corner.

"It doesn't go any faster!" said Lamp.

"It did on the way."

"I don't know what's wrong. We're slowing down!" Lamp tussled violently with the golf club and the buggy emitted a *GRRAUNCH* noise, followed by something not unlike an elephant hiccupping. Lamp banged his hand against the toilet seat. "No, no, no, no!"

Casper couldn't handle the tension. "What is it, *what is it?*"

"I think all that coriander clogged up the engine."

"Clogged it up?"

Lamp pointed to a calculator on the dashboard. "What does it say?"

"Four."

"Four?"

"Yeah. Is that bad?"

"I don't know. It's only ever said three before!"

The buggy rattled turbulently and both the boys were shaken from their seats. With an angry spit, the engine emitted its last squeeze of lemon-fresh fuel and died. The buggy rolled idly into a patch of wild strawberries on the roadside and the world went silent.

"I'm sorry," said Lamp, head bowed.

"It's all right," Casper replied with a heavy sigh. "It got us this far."

Casper turned to look at his best friend. Lamp's hair

was matted and dirty, his boiler suit was covered in oil and soap, and two cheeky toes were poking through the end of his left sponge shoe. He may not have been perfect, but Lamp Flannigan was all that Casper had.

Neither of them spoke for a long time. The moon shone softly down on the wrecked buggy, while the clock ticked itself steadily onwards (at the speed of about one second per second) towards midnight. The boys had no ride home, no way to save Julius, and all they wanted was to curl up in bed and go to sleep.

"What now?" said Casper.

"Ooh, I know!" said Lamp, eyes lighting up. "I spy with my little eye, something beginning with five."

"Shh, what's that noise?"

"That doesn't start with a five."

"No, no, Lamp, listen."

Lamp closed his eyes and cocked his head. In the

silence Casper could definitely hear a noise: a sort of low rumbling, like Mayor Rattsbulge's belly before dinner. Gradually the noise grew more defined, louder, more rumbly, until it shook the ground beneath them.

"Oh, no," said Lamp, face filled with horror. "I've seen this in a film. It's dinosaurs."

The sound got rumblier. Casper shook his head and laughed. Surely it couldn't be dinosaurs; they didn't hang around in the Kobb Valley, did they? Did they? "Oh, golly," he said, "it's dinosaurs."

The rumble was more of a thunder now, a really rumbly thunder. The rumbliest thunder you'll ever hear, in fact (unless you attended the International Rumbly Thunder Festival in Madrid back in 1963, but you didn't because I just made it up). The boys jumped down from the buggy and peered over the dusky horizon, but they saw nothing.

"Stay still," whispered Casper. "They can't see you if you stay still."

"I'm scared," said Lamp, trembling.

The ground shuddered violently, shaking the trees loose of apples, conkers and

sleepy owls, which tumbled to the ground and hooted off. (Only the owls hooted off – conkers and apples generally don't hoot very much).

Then, from behind the next hill, Casper saw a dark shape appear, sort of like a top hat. As the hat rose higher, Casper could see that it was attached to a man, and the man was attached to some sort of beast, and the beast was attached to some sort of legs, which were running towards them rather fast.

But the hat/man/beast/legs weren't alone. More shapes appeared beside it, and then more still, all rumbling in their direction at a blistering speed.

"That's not dinosaurs," Lamp clapped his hands and wiggled. "It's him! It's The Great Tickertape!"

Casper could make out his face now. Lamp was right! Riding on the back of his majestic white tiger was The Great Tiramisu himself, with his purple cape back on, but still without any trousers, whooping and cheering and waving his arms around. He was flanked by the Shetland pony and the walrus – and also the two swordfish, belly-down on skateboards. The rabbits and beavers gaily bounded in and out of the larger animals' legs, and swooping about in the air were the doves, cooing with glee. And they all still sported their purple bow ties, top hats and bristling fake moustaches.

Casper rubbed his eyes; he couldn't believe what he was seeing. He half expected to see the dinosaurs come trundling over the hill behind them.

The Great Tiramisu reined the white tiger to a halt as he reached the boys. "You *bambini* need-a the lift?"

"I… uhh…" Casper was struggling to find any words to say, let alone appropriate ones. "What are you doing?"

"I have seen the error of my-a ways," said The Great Tiramisu, smoothing his moustache with a manicured finger. "I was a bad-a man. Bad-a to you,

bad-a to my beasties, bad-a to everybody. But now, we make it all-a better!" He broke into a graceful smile. "Now, we go save-a your papa. Jump on!"

Casper, still in disbelief, clambered on to the back of the Shetland pony, while Lamp leapt on to the walrus. The Great Tiramisu whistled

and the flotilla of performing animals rumbled onwards, Casper and Lamp now on board, off to face whatever horrors lay ahead in Corne-on-the-Kobb.

Chapter 15

Do Not Feed the Pigeons

Casper clung on to the Shetland pony's mane as she jostled him about on her back, little stocky legs galloping away like clumsy sausages. He managed to pump the air with his fist and shout "Woohoo!" before he lost his balance and almost fell off, at which point he grabbed her mane with both hands and wished he'd brought a saddle or some glue.

By the looks of it, Lamp was having an even tougher time on the back of the walrus. He'd gripped on to his tusks, and as he flopped down the road, Lamp was repeatedly thrown upwards and then smacked back down, each time getting a faceful of fishy skin and a catalogue of bruises. The walrus didn't care – he was barking with delight and bounding as high as his flippers would spring him, which was all the more painful for Lamp. Perhaps a ride on the back of a swordfish would've been smoother (if a little more fishy).

And then there was The Great Tiramisu. Casper had never seen him like this. He rode the white tiger joyfully, giggling like Betty Woons in a jelly-bean factory. This wasn't the same pompous magician that Casper and Lamp had met that fateful night – he *had* changed, his inner idiot had been released.

"No more-a magic for-a me," The Great Tiramisu called over the thundering of hooves, flippers, paws and skateboards. "I learnt something today. The bubbles, you *bambini*... it is better to-a have *fun*!"

Before long they were just a couple of miles out from Corne-on-the-Kobb, but the poor walrus was struggling to keep up. His flippers sagged and he grunted wearily at every step. (Walruses aren't very good at running at the best of times. Did you know that not one walrus has ever completed the London marathon? Well, one did, but he took the bus.) The beavers too had given up and hopped on top of the two swordfish and were now riding them like a Viking longboat.

"Come on," cried Casper, "we haven't got long!" And, as they neared the village, familiar dark clouds gathered, obscuring the moonlight, and the rain started to patter down.

"The curse, it not-a lift!" The Great Tiramisu swizzled his moustache and frowned (which is what Italian men with moustaches do when they are worried that their curses haven't lifted).

The further they went, the heavier the rain fell. Soon the animals were sloshing through ankle-deep puddles, making things easier for the swordfish, the walrus and also the rabbits who, luckily, had been learning breaststroke, but much harder for everybody else. Lightning struck a tree a few fields away, the thunder was massive and deafening. The Shetland pony whinnied and reared up, again almost throwing Casper off, but he clung on like a tic on the ankle of a particularly delicious chocolate Labrador. The doves spun and wheeled manically, agitated by the rain, but still they all pushed on.

They passed what used to be Sandy Landscape's front garden, where the cabbages now resembled seaweed and the moles had installed a diving board. Lightning struck again, closer this time.

"Nearly there!" Casper shouted.

They passed Lamp's house, garage door still open, its contents completely drowned (apart from the hamster, who had a snorkel).

Casper could make out the sound of people shouting up ahead. "Can you hear that?" he called over the rain.

Lamp stuck his ear out. "What is it?"

"A crowd! We might not be too late!"

As they turned the final corner towards the village square the waters became shallower, which stranded the swordfish (who had long since dumped their skateboards). The Great Tiramisu spurred the white tiger for one last sprint. Casper could hear the crowd more distinctly. They were chanting something, but he couldn't make it out over the rain.

The villagers were in sight now, a sea of savage idiots in anoraks and duffel coats, lit by the flicker of a hundred flaming torches, driven wild by the thrill of a good old public execution. The Great Tiramisu's raggedy gang reached the square and the little beavers collapsed with exhaustion.

"Go!" The Great Tiramisu shouted. "Go and-a save your papa!"

Leaping off their sweaty steeds, the boys sprinted towards the vast pigeon cage in the centre where the statue had once stood, surrounded by the pack of frenzied villagers.

Casper glanced up at the village hall clock. "Quarter to eleven!" he shouted to Lamp over the din. "We've got loads of time."

"No you ain't," bellowed Sandy Landscape, who was standing near the back of the crowd, pitchfork in hand. "The mayor brung it forward to get 'ome for 'is midnight feast. We're doin' it now."

"What? Now?" The boys shared a look of horror and charged forward through the throng, desperate to save Julius. Inside the cage the pigeons flapped about wildly, provoked by the crowd and the rain, and hungry for flesh. Casper elbowed past Anemonie Blight, perched on her mother's pointy shoulders. Anemonie's face, lit only by the licking flames of the torches, was painted with streaks of red and her squinty eyes looked particularly savage. She cackled wildly and flapped her arms like wings, pecking the air. Then, with horror, they saw Julius. Arms and legs in chains, he was being shoved out of the darkness towards the cage by the crowd of bloaty-faced idiots, followed by the fatter-than-ever Mayor Rattsbulge, in full mayoral gowns (made of six pairs of curtains and some string). People were pelting pigeon feed at Julius, and Casper now clearly heard the chanting:

"Peck him! Peck him! Peck him!"

"Stop! Stop! The curse has been lifted!" Casper yelled, reaching the front of the surging crowd, but they weren't listening any more. Julius didn't struggle; he let them lug him forward. They reached the cast-iron door and Mayor Rattsbulge fumbled with the padlock in the pelting rain. As Julius looked helplessly to the crowd, Casper met his eyes.

"Dad!" he shouted.

Julius was shocked.

"Casper?"

"Dad, I'm sorry!" Casper tried to run forward, but was held back. "I tried so hard! I'm sorry!"

"It's all right, Casp," Julius answered calmly. "I know. Look after Amanda and Cuddles. Tell them I love them." The padlock clicked open. "Be a good boy."

The cage swung wide; the villagers shoved Julius in.

"*No!*" Casper cried.

The crowd fell silent, silent as a mouse that was allergic to its own squeak. Julius watched the pigeons. The pigeons watched Julius. Betty Woons watched the news. (She had forgotten to come.) One of the pigeons made a *Coo* noise. The crowd gasped. Another pigeon pecked at the ground. The crowd gasped again and Clemmie Answorth fell off her chair (which she'd brought along, just in case she needed to fall off it). A fat pigeon waddled about a bit. Many of the women screamed, the rest of the crowd just gasped again.

"What's happnin'?" demanded Sandy Landscape, struggling to see from deep within the crowd.

"Nothing!" said Audrey Snugglepuss from right at the front. (She'd camped in the square since lunchtime for a good seat.)

A few murmurs of disappointment spread through the mob.

Anemonie Blight was getting impatient. "Go on, pigeons! Tasty man-meat!" she spat. "Peck him!"

"Peck him! Peck him!" shouted the crowd. But the pigeons obviously weren't hungry. Either that, or they didn't understand English because they waddled around, doing pigeonish things and, most importantly, not eating Julius.

Julius looked through the bars at Casper and forced a nervous smile. Casper stuck both thumbs up and grinned back.

"I think it's working," Lamp whispered.

Even as Lamp spoke, Casper noticed the monsoon lighten to a mere deluge.

Sandy Landscape looked to the sky and said, "It's stoppin' rainin'!"

"And the pigeons aren't hungry," said Audrey Snugglepuss. The crowd was stirring. She was right – the pigeons were merrily minding their own business, steering well clear of Julius Candlewacks. The rain had almost completely subsided and the clouds were parting to reveal a shining full moon.

Mrs Snagg felt her face. "My spots… they've gone."

The villagers looked around at one another and agreed that there had been a considerable downturn in pustular ubiquity (although they didn't use those words). Their murmur had swelled to a feverish chatter. Mayor Rattsbulge looked from the cage to the sky and finally to his villagers. "It can't be…" he said in disbelief. "The curse… It's… *it's gone!*"

On hearing this announcement, the village erupted with triumphant cheers; men and women alike embraced the closest person to hand; the emotional among them burst into tears of relief, and a hastily prepared brass band played a joyful tune.

Casper put his arm round Lamp's shoulder and closed his eyes. "We did it, Lamp."

Mayor Rattsbulge, who had been vigorously shaking hands with anyone who had a hand free, prepared to make an announcement. "Ladies and

gentlemen," he boomed. "To the pub!"

The crowd cheered again and three burly men attempted to lift the mayor into the air. They buckled under the weight of his monumental frame and a few more came to help. Eventually, after a few broken spines and the use of a rudimentary winch-and-pulley system, Mayor Rattsbulge was hoisted shakily above the crowd, and another triumphant cheer rang out.

They marched off, carrying their rotund hero towards
The Horse and Horse, accompanied by the brass band,
leaving Julius with the pigeons inside the cage.

Casper walked over to his father. "You OK?"

"Yeah," Julius replied. "I'm alive. I think."

They both laughed, and then Julius said, "Can you
let me out of here?"

Casper had no problem opening the padlock –
Mayor Rattsbulge had left the key in. Julius, hands and
feet still in manacles, shuffled out of the cage. Casper
hugged his father, reunited at last.

"I'm sorry, Dad," he said. "It was my fault."

"It doesn't matter, Casp. The pigeons didn't eat me,

and by the looks of it, you had something to do with that." Julius ruffled his son's hair.

"You couldn't have done it without my buggy!" said Lamp.

"Not without *you*, Lamp," said Casper. "You and me, we saved the day."

Lamp straightened his boiler suit and grinned to himself. He'd never saved the day before, but it felt nice; so he made a mental note to do it again sometime, next time the day needed saving.

"Isn't that…" Julius had spotted The Great Tiramisu and his soggy pets, heaped over at the entrance to the square. "What's *he* doing here?"

"It's fine!" said Casper. "He's had a change of heart."

The Great Tiramisu waved. "Is OK, I no bad-a man no more."

"Where are his trousers?" asked Julius.

"Long story, Dad," said Casper, laughing.

Clambering back on the white tiger, The Great Tiramisu straightened his top hat. "I must go."

"Where?"

"Who-a knows? We will explore-a de world."

"And you'll not go back to how you were?"

"Never. I learn today that life is for-a having fun. I never go back." The Great Tiramisu gave the white tiger a tickle and she purred. Then he pulled up his Y-fronts and shouted, "Yee-haa!" and rode off into the night, with his gang of merry animals fluttering, scampering, galloping and flopping behind.

"We'll miss you, Great Tomato!" shouted Lamp, waving them off.

Casper, Lamp and Julius stood in the moonlit square for a long time, just smiling at each other. Back in the cage the pigeons doddered around; a sprig of coriander rode on a gust of wind before flopping into a puddle, and off in the pub a toast was being proposed to the saviour of the day, Mayor Ignatius P. Rattsbulge.

"Come on, boys, let's go home and see if we can't get these chains off, eh?" said Julius, holding up his cuffed hands and smiling.

"I made some acid out of sherbet lemons," said Lamp. "We could try that."

"Yeah, why not?" said Casper.

The three of them clanked off home, leaving behind all the idiots and the coriander and the pigeons because, in the end, you don't really need idiots or coriander, or even pigeons. In the end, all you really need in life is a buggy that runs on washing-up liquid and a couple of boys to crash it.

Epilogue

The moonlight shone over Corne-on-the-Kobb. On Cracklin Crescent the old oak tree was far sprightlier than it had looked over the past few days, and the floodwaters were fast subsiding. Casper and Lamp splashed down the street, with Julius jangling about not far back.

"Ahh, home," sang Julius, taking a deep breath of the cool night air. "It'll feel so good to get these chains off."

Casper chortled and swung his arms around. "Yeah, I bet Mum and… oh, no."

"What is it?" asked Lamp, worried.

Casper's face was leaden. "Mum and Cuddles. We left them alone all evening!"

"Oh, lord." said Julius, lifting his heavy manacled hand to his mouth.

"Who will have fed Cuddles? Who will have changed its nappy?" Casper and Lamp were running now, with Julius clanking along frantically behind. Casper reached the porch, heart beating like a pneumatic drill.

Nothing out of the ordinary. No crying.

He pressed the doorbell. No answer. What had happened? Julius had arrived now and he pressed the doorbell again. Still no answer. Casper thought he heard a bump from inside. Where was Amanda? He couldn't hear the TV. Where was Cuddles? He couldn't hear any screams. Casper was now banging on the door and shouting through the letterbox.

Some steps. The door clicked open.

What greeted Casper was something he'd never seen before, not even in his dreams; something he didn't expect ever to see at all. Standing at the door was Amanda Candlewacks, all tender and motherly, with Cuddles in her arms, happily gnawing on a hairbrush. Casper looked round at Julius. He too was lost for words.

Amanda blinked, taking in her first sight of the outdoors for years, and then smiled at her husband, her son and his friend. Then she looked down at Cuddles.

She smiled again. "It's a girl!"

Acknowledgments:

There are an awful lot of idiots I need to thank, starting with my mother, my greyhound, and the rest of my lovely family. Thanks to my guinea-pig-readers, Sevi, Tom and Frederick; to my ever-supportive agent Eve White; to my marvellous editor Harriet Wilson and all the idiots at HarperCollins; and to Amy, the biggest idiot of them all.

CASPER CANDLEWACKS

in the CLAWS of CRIME!

Ivan Brett

When a crime wave sweeps over

Corne-on-the-Kobb baffling everyone in its path,

it's up to Casper to catch the crook and

save the day.

ISBN: 978-0-00-741157-3

Out in January 2012

Read on for a sneak preview

The alarm didn't wake Mayor Rattsbulge at first; he just wiped the dribble off his chin, grunted and rolled over. He was having a cracking dream about hog-roasts, and really didn't want to wake up before he'd reached the apple sauce. But then the noise seeped through the non-food part of his brain (a tiny section squeezed away behind the locum hamburgarium) and he leapt out of bed like he was covered in bees. He threw on his extra-large dressing gown and blundered out of his extra-large bedroom on to the pitch-black landing, tripping over the banister and tumbling down the stairs. He bounced at the bottom (thanks to his six bowls of jelly for pudding) and landed rather gracefully on his blubbery feet. Mayor Rattsbulge rushed out of the front door, stopping only to grab a Cumberland sausage from the jar on the hall table. It took him a good three minutes to heave himself to the other side of the lamp-lit village square, where a small crowd of villagers in their pyjamas had gathered by the door to the village vault.

Audrey Snugglepuss, the village gossip and baker of cakes, strode forward angrily and flicked her nightcap out of her face. "For crying out loud, Mayor Rattsbulge, I'm trying to sleep," she warbled.

"Hear hear," sung Clemmie Answorth, a slightly younger, nervous looking woman completely peppered with bruises, and still clutching her teddy. "What with all that racket, I fell out of my bed." She did that a lot.

Mayor Rattsbulge wheezed and clutched his chest. "Ladies, please," He leant on a lamppost but it buckled under his weight. "I've only just got here. Now, what's the alarm?"

Mitch McMassive, the tiny landlord of village pub 'The Horse and Horse' and star striker in his local Table Football team, stuck his little hand in the air and squeaked, "Look, Mayor." He trotted forward to the heavy wooden door and gave its brass handle an almighty shove. It groaned open groggily on its rusty hinges. "Someone's broken the lock."

The bolder villagers bundled through the door into the blackness, and tripped straight over an empty wheelchair.

Clemmie Answorth screeched and tinkled through a glass cabinet, while all around dull thuds told stories of foreheads meeting walls and coming off the worse.

Audrey Snugglepuss fumbled for a light switch in the dark. Her first attempt found Mitch McMassive's button nose, which snicked out of joint at the slightest press and failed to make the room any lighter. Her second attempt got Mitch's nose again with similar, squealier results. Her third attempt at last found the switch and the vault was plunged into dazzling amber light.

"My nose!" honked Mitch McMassive through a crimson torrent running down his face. "I can smell blood."

Betty Woons blinked awake and chuckled at all of the bodies rolling around her.

"Oh hello dears," she warbled. "What are we all doing on the floor? Sleepover, is it?"

Mayor Rattsbulge was the first to notice. "Oh, my sweet lord…" he whispered, prodding a trembling finger towards the cabinet. A few silent moments passed as the villagers rubbed the glare from their eyes and spotted the empty space where the sword used to be.

The mayor swallowed, shaking from head to toe. "It's… gone…"

Clemmie Answorth spluttered. "The sword's gone?"

"Who used it last?"

"Well, I didn't take it," said Audrey Snugglepuss

"What about my nose?" squeaked Mitch McMassive.

"Anyone for jelly beans?" asked Betty Woons.

"SHUT UP!" bellowed the Mayor. "Shut up and find it. Find my sword!"

The pyjama-clad crowd screamed and ran out into the moonlit square, searching under doormats and tipping over flowerpots. Meanwhile, back in the vault, village gardener Sandy Landscape (who'd watched *three whole* detective shows on telly so he knew what he was talking about) edged closer to the cabinet. "'Ere… Mayor…"

"What is it?" sobbed Mayor Rattsbulge from behind his gravy-stained hanky.

"I found summink. Look yer eyes on that." Sandy's grubby fingers reached into the cabinet and pulled out something black and wiry. He held it to the light, and gasped.

It was a single cat's whisker.